The world can't get enough of Miss Seeton

"A **most beguiling** protagonist!"
New York Times

Miss Seeton gets into wild drama with fine touches of farce … This is a **lovely mixture of the funny and the exciting**."
San Francisco Chronicle

"This is not so much black comedy as black-currant comedy … **You can't stop reading. Or laughing.**"
The Sun

Depth of description and lively characters bring this English village to life."
Publishers Weekly

"Fun to be had with a **full cast of endearingly zany villagers** … and the ever gently intuitive Miss Seeton."
Kirkus Reviews

s Seeton is the **most delightfully satisfactory character since Miss Marple.**"
Ogden Nash

"**She's a joy!**"
Cleveland Plain Dealer

Miss Seeton Draws the Line

A MISS SEETON MYSTERY

Heron Carvic

This edition published in 2017 by Farrago, an imprint of
Prelude Books Ltd
13 Carrington Road, Richmond, TW10 5AA, United Kingdom

www.farragobooks.com

First published by Geoffrey Bles in 1969

Copyright © The Beneficiaries of the Literary Estate of
Heron Carvic 2017

The right of Heron Carvic to be identified as the author of this Work has been asserted by him in accordance with the Copyright, Designs & Patents Act 1988.

All rights reserved. No part of this publication may be reproduced, stored in a retrieval system, or transmitted, in any form or by any means, without the prior permission in writing of the publisher.

This book is a work of fiction. Names, characters, businesses, organizations, places and events other than those clearly in the public domain, are either the product of the author's imagination or are used fictitiously. Any resemblance to actual persons, living or dead, events or locales is entirely coincidental.

ISBN: 978-1-911440-55-0

NORTH AYRSHIRE
LIBRARIES
07357060
Bertrams 14/03/2017
£7.99
L
CANCELLED

Have you read them all?

Treat yourself again to the first Miss Seeton novels—

Picture Miss Seeton
A night at the opera strikes a chord of danger when Miss Seeton witnesses a murder … and paints a portrait of the killer.

Miss Seeton Draws the Line
Miss Seeton is enlisted by Scotland Yard when her paintings of a little girl turn the young subject into a model for murder.

Witch Miss Seeton
Double, double, toil and trouble sweep through the village when Miss Seeton goes undercover … to investigate a local witches' coven!

Turn to the end of this book for a full list of the series, plus—on the last page—**exclusive access to the Miss Seeton short story** that started it all.

For Viola and Phoebe

Chapter 1

"Stop!"

The little girl took no notice and stepped into the road. Miss Seeton ran forward, lunged, hooked her umbrella handle round the endangered child's arm, yanked, and the little girl sat down hard on the cement curb that bordered the grass shoulder as the car halted with a jerk inches from her feet. She shrugged free of the umbrella and raised her eyes to her rescuer.

"Silly ol' cow," said the endangered child.

"Effie," a woman yelled from across the road, "come 'ere at once an' if I catch you trying to kill yerself again I'll do yer an' that's a promise."

The squat little figure got to its feet and stamped toward its home.

"An' mind yer manners," her mother admonished her. "Say thank yer an' ye're sorry."

The child turned, looked at the car, at Miss Seeton, stuck out her tongue, turned back, and went into the house.

"Thank yer," called her mother, "and I'm sorry for yer trouble but there y'are I can't do nothing with her." She followed her daughter. The front door slammed.

Miss Seeton turned to the driver with a smile, "Children—so thoughtless. Though not all," she admitted. "Some are very good. They teach them, you know, in school. There are classes, with lollipops—those men with white coats and poles with a disk on top to lead them, like Roman legionaires. Only sometimes they forget. The children, I mean. It was wonderful that you stopped so quickly. There might," she explained, "have been an accident."

Two impassive faces stared toward her. The driver, a boy; clean hair clubbed, a rough fringe across his forehead, clear skin, a sullen face with waiting, wary eyes. His passenger, a girl; brushed hair hanging loose, an apathetic countenance, the eyes fearful. Neither spoke. Miss Seeton smiled again and stepped back. The boy engaged gear. The car moved.

Miss Seeton watched it drive away. The young. So shy.

She glanced across at the neat row of council houses before continuing down the Street to her cottage. Effie Goffer. Not, one must admit, an attractive subject. Nor, one feared, very well mannered. But for Mrs. Goffer's sake she would try again. Yes. After lunch she would get out her drawing things. Just because her first attempt had been a lamentable failure was no reason … After all, ugly ducklings. Miss Seeton's imagination strained to picture Effie as swan material; another lamentable failure. The Frog Prince, perhaps. But then the sex was wrong. Except, of course, in Pantomime. Such a pity that she was no good at the type of portrait where you just drew a cube and stuck eyes in it. Miss Seeton smiled; then felt guilty. A cube, with eyes, was, one had to confess, a very apt description of Effie.

By the time Miss Seeton reached her gate she had solved her problem. Not a straight portrait at all. Something allegorical and rather pretty, with only just a suggestion of Effie. That was the answer.

It was very worrying.

She considered the drawing on her desk.

Not allegorical. And certainly not pretty. In fact it was quite dreadful and—and shocking. Her shoulders contracted to a cold sensation in her spine. She threw down her crayon. Really this was too childish. She would be getting fanciful next. Put the whole thing out of her mind for a moment and think of something else. Something pleasant. She pushed the drawing block to one side, turned her chair, and looked out the French window.

To see the buds breaking; that tender green haze forming like mist on bare branches. Crocus, primrose, daffodil … Green and yellow—the flag of youth; the aching cry of innocence. So many writers had grown lyrical over spring. And, one must admit, it was easy to love a lamb: but how soon that engaging frivolity would yield to the placid idiocy of its inheritance; it was not easy to love a sheep. Summer? Yes, but it was overweighted, overcolored. No—for herself she preferred late autumn, when line returned, with wider, subtler blends of color and experience. And faith fulfilled or dead. Probably it was one's age.

Hers was a gentle view. The garden sloped down to the Royal Military Canal which, in spite of its imposing title, is for much of its length little more than a grandiose ditch. Beyond the trees bordering the canal the fields of Kent stretched flat to the coast, Rye to the west, New Romney to the east.

She returned to her drawing block, removed the top sheet, laid it aside, picked up a soft pencil, arranged her crayons.

She would try again. It was ridiculous to imagine there was anything wrong. It was simply lack of concentration. She must concentrate.

She concentrated.

She studied the result.

Oh dear. Really it was very worrying. This was her third attempt. And it was no better.

She took the two previous drawings and laid all three in a row on the flap of the writing desk. With plain sheets of paper she covered the right-hand half of each sketch: three semiportraits of the same little girl; the same lank hair, the same fat cheek, the same shoebutton eye, the same sly lift to the corner of the mouth, the same olive complexion. She moved the covering sheets to reveal the other half of the face: the same blurred, uncertain outline, the same slit, half-open eye, the same droop to the corner of the mouth, the same greenish-blue coloring. The same death mask. Removing the top sheets, she left the three drawings exposed. Individually each was disturbing: viewed in triplicate they were macabre.

What was she to do? After all, she was, she supposed, in a certain sense committed to making a sketch of Effie for Mrs. Goffer. Not a direct promise, of course—Miss Seeton was beginning to learn that such transactions were never direct in a small village like Plummergen. In fact it had been Martha's suggestion. In a way, that was. When she had finished cleaning the cottage the other week Martha had mentioned, just before leaving, that she had met Mrs. Goffer while shopping and that Mrs. Goffer had let fall that she wouldn't mind, not really, if someone did a drawing of little Effie, couldn't really see no harm in it, and her own opinion, Martha's opinion, was, well, why not?

Three good reasons why not now lay upon her desk.

She couldn't possibly allow Mrs. Goffer to see one of these. They were—well, they were horrid. The likeness was there, she had to admit. But, in a way, that was a disadvantage. Because, as again one had to admit, little Effie Goffer was a distressingly plain child. There was no doubt that she did feel under a certain obligation to Mrs. Goffer. It had been kind of her, in these days when it was almost impossible to get daily help, to come in twice a week for the fortnight that Martha had been away. Slapdash, perhaps, but none the less kind. And then, during the three days when one had been suffering from that bad cold, Mrs. Goffer, although so much younger, had been almost embarrassingly maternal; insisting that one should stay in bed, doing all the shopping, and coming round in the evening to cook supper, which one did not want, and to change one's hot-water bottle, which one did. Such cosseting, although irritating, had been well meant and, in the event, awkward because Mrs. Goffer had refused any extra money for these services, saying that it were a bit of a do if neighbors couldn't help each other out when poorly. And Mrs. Goffer was not even a neighbor since she lived at the other end of the village. All in all one was left with the feeling that one would be grateful for the opportunity to do something in return—that one owed Mrs. Goffer something. Certainly—she contemplated the three sketches—something better than this. Each time she had tried the left-hand side of the face—actually, of course, in Effie herself it would be the right-hand side—had come easily enough with no trouble. But when it came to the right side—that would be Effie's left—well, the first time, when she had had Effie here for a sitting, for which her mother had crimped, starched, and overdressed the child almost beyond recognition and certainly beyond suitability, she hadn't noticed anything wrong until afterwards, when Effie had demanded to see her picture. Fortunately one had instinctively sat back to judge it for oneself first, and there had just been time to cover it and explain that it was only a beginning and would have to be worked on before anyone could see it. Effie had been insistent and a little rude and one had had to be firm. And also quite firm that no further sitting would be necessary. Indeed, in view of the result, she had felt that it would be safer, when trying again, to do so from memory. On her second and third attempts she had paid particular attention—her hand seemed to slow down, the fingers growing almost numb, and her arm became leaden and sluggish. And she had found herself compelled—yes, quite literally compelled—to pick up the wrong colors in the crayons. Could it be, she wondered, something in herself? It was so much better, when one was a little distressed, to face the matter and put it into words.

She straightened in her chair; prepared to face the matter; to put it into words.

Could she have had …? Should she, perhaps, ask Dr. Knight? He might be able to advise her or suggest some form of treatment if she really had had a … This was ridiculous.

She picked up a pencil and wrote in courageous capitals on a sheet of paper STROKE.

There. That was better. Now it was out and one could face it properly. Because if one had had one, she looked at the written word before her and nodded to it, however slight—and at one's age it would be perfectly understandable—then, surely, it would show in other ways as well. As one wouldn't be able to do all the things one did. With regard to her hands and arms alone, it was only in the past week or two that she had been able to achieve the Cow-Face Posture, such a very odd description, from that clever book *Yoga and Younger Every Day* which had helped her so much. Because, if there was any lack of coordination between her brain and her right arm, she didn't see how she could manage to put one arm behind her back and the other over her head and then grip the hands in the middle of her back and remain there doing deep breathing. No, really, now that she faced it openly, she didn't see how it could be—what she'd written. But, all the same, she considered the drawings again, there was something wrong. She would ring up Dr. Knight and ask if he would be kind enough to see her.

She gathered the sketches and placed them in a folder. Before closing it she once more examined the top portrait. She shook her head.

Really, it was very worrying indeed.

Detective Superintendent Delphick finished his examination kneeling on the damp grass and rose.

"All right. Take him away."

He walked from the lighted area, through the misty twilight and the comparative gloom of the street lamps, to the road. The ambulance men bent down under the arc lights. The muttering of the crowd behind the police cordon swelled. A woman at the back cried out:

"Why'n't you do something? Why'n't you stop it? How many …?"

She broke off as Delphick's face, eyes unfocused, turned toward her. The crowd became silent. A press photographer lowered his camera; not the moment. The inspector in charge from the Lewisham Division, who had moved forward to speak, halted and left it unsaid. The silence lasted until the superintendent had got into his car.

Sergeant Ranger, following his superior from the corner of the children's playground, stopped to watch them lift the body of the twelve-year-old boy and lay a blanket over the stretcher, covering the scraped shoes, the knees and shorts grimed with soil, the jersey snagged with dead twigs from the bush under which he had been found, the swollen face.

"The Oracle's taking it hard, isn't he?" commented the Lewisham inspector. Sergeant Ranger nodded. "Of course," continued the inspector, "this is only our first. For him it makes just one more to add to the collection."

The sergeant nodded again. "Looks like something's biting him. If you'll carry on with the routine. Inspector, we'll be in touch."

The sergeant reached the police car, jackknifed his huge frame into the driving seat, and slammed the door.

"The Yard," said Delphick.

Back in their office the sergeant transcribed his notes.

There hadn't been time to gather much: Lawrence Massyn, aged twelve years three months. Body discovered 4:15 P.M. approx. by children using playground. Body apparently been dragged under a … He contemplated his shorthand. Under a hypodermic? Couldn't be. Hyperic? Hysteric? Could be anything. Perhaps the Oracle … He stole a glance toward the superintendent's desk.

Delphick sat motionless, his gaze fixed on a glass case screwed to the wall. It was such a case as a fisherman might have in which to display his greatest catch. Unobservant visitors over the past few months had been left with the impression that the superintendent devoted his leisure to angling for fish in complement to his daily routine of entangling men. In fact the case contained a broken umbrella. It also held a memory for Delphick: not of a catch, but a reminder of a failure to do so and that, although an arrest had finally been made, it had been through another's luck, not through his own judgment.

The sergeant reverted to his hieroglyphics. Not the moment to ask the Oracle for nature notes. Under a—bush, he decided. With leaves, he added. Some of the other bushes round the playground had hardly got any leaves yet, so perhaps hyper-whoosit was botanical for leafy. He finished his transcription and made a note: check fog time. Up here it had started to clear soon after two o'clock so the killing had probably been done before then. But it might have been different down Lewisham way. He'd check when they got back there. Back there? They should never have left. He'd never known the Oracle do this—walk out on a case without a word. Ought he to remind him? Well—no. You didn't remind the Oracle of things. And certainly not in this mood. Quite the opposite actually. He usually reminded you. Lewisham? What the devil was it about Lewisham? Something or other.

The sergeant started as the superintendent suddenly reached for a telephone.

"Chief Superintendent Gosslin, please." … "Chief?" … "Delphick here." … "Yes." … Yes—and I should be there but—" … "Please." … "Right. Right away." The superintendent replaced the receiver and left the office.

The sergeant watched him go. The Oracle couldn't be pulling out? Asking to be taken off? Well, he meant, you didn't. Even when a case was up the spout and hell on castors like this one, you—you just didn't. He leaned down, pulled out a bottom drawer of his desk, and withdrew a stack of files.

He selected four. This new one at Lewisham certainly looked like one of the Oracle's specials. What had got into people? Granted crime went in waves and fashions—always had—but this child murder business was getting overdone altogether. Anyway, where was the point in it? Nothing to gain or anything. What'd they got? Fifteen—and today's made sixteen—in roughly two years. And only about half of them solved. Of course a lot of them were sex ones—and with small children that really did seem a bit off. The sergeant grimaced. Well, he meant, what could you ...? Oh well, skip it.

He spread out the four files on cases when a similarity of method had been noted, cases which had become Superintendent Delphick's particular headache. The sergeant took an empty folder and labeled it LEWISHAM. He frowned. Lewisham? Something about Lewisham. He glanced at the labels on the other files. Brentwood, Richmond, Wimbledon, West Malling. Three in or around London and one down in Kent near Maidstone—what had made him pop down there all of a sudden?—and now back up to Lewisham. What was it about Lewisham? Something he'd read or somebody'd said. Oh yes, of course, in the canteen. Somebody'd been talking about a raid on a subpost office in Lewisham. Well, that was the hell of a help. All the teeners were cutting their teeth nowadays on subpost offices before promoting themselves to the man-sized jobs like banks and trains. Three boys, one girl—at least he didn't play favorites—ages varying between ten and fourteen. And now another boy, at Lewisham. So it was the odds the next might be a girl. All strangled. All for no reason that anybody could see. Just put the mug on 'em and rabbit. Pretty rough. No wonder the press had got the jitters and was screaming. Several of the papers had run articles by psychiatrists telling the police what type to look for. That was the hell of a help, too. It gave the police several types to look for. As if they didn't know that what they'd got to look for was somebody who'd flipped his wig. What nobody seemed to realize was that wig-flipping didn't show—not until they'd got to the "I'm an egg looking for a pan to fry in" stage.

The sergeant jostled the files together and slammed them down on the side of the desk.

What could you do when you were up against a madman? How did you get a clue to somebody who was off his tot unless you actually caught him at it? Nothing to get hold of; no sex; no robbery; no reason; nothing. What, repeat what, could you do?

"What could she do?" Sir Hubert Everleigh, Assistant Commissioner, C.I.D., went on before Delphick could answer: "If we are to entertain, or even to evaluate, this suggestion of yours, a suggestion which I may say is unique in my experience, if, to summarize, the police are to admit defeat and hand over the case to the general public." Delphick opened his mouth to protest. "Or, to be more exact," Sir Hubert corrected himself, "to one member of the public, I feel constrained to ask, although I agree with Euripides that Providence has many different aspects, what particular aspect are we to look for in an elderly drawing mistress? What, I repeat, to be precise, could she do?"

Chief Superintendent Gosslin, present as always at such a conference to act as a buffer for his subordinates, tried to give Delphick time to collect his thoughts. He grunted.

The assistant commissioner ignored him and continued to watch Delphick with inquiry.

How the hell, thought Delphick, did you explain to the A.C. thoughts and feelings that were so vague that you had difficulty in putting them into words for yourself? The chief knew him. They'd worked together long enough, trusted each other, and old Gosslin would always let him have his head to a reasonable extent without having to dot all the "i's" or cross every little "t." But that wasn't going to do here. The A.C. was determined to probe.

"I'm afraid it's very nebulous, sir," he began.

"Feelings always are," agreed the assistant commissioner. "Nebulous as in the work of Gerard Croiset?"

Delphick was so taken aback that he gasped. Be double damned. Realizing that he was gaping like a freshly landed cod, he laughed.

"You find the analogy amusing?"

"No, sir, far from it. It was the surprise at finding you ahead of me when I was still groping for words to explain."

Gosslin cleared his throat. "Well, speaking for myself, I'm not even under starter's orders. Who's this Gerard Whoosit, sir? Never heard of him."

"No reason why you should," replied Sir Hubert. "He's a Dutch clairvoyant, medium, or whatever you like to call it, who's consulted a lot by the Continental police on tricky cases!" Gosslin snorted. "Of course we don't go in for that sort of thing here, not officially. We don't believe in it, or say we don't." He returned to Delphick. "It was some drawings which she did during a case in which she got involved accidentally last year that gave you this idea, I understand."

"Yes, sir. Though, unlike Croiset, in Miss Seeton's case I think it's more or less unconscious. I imagine she would be most indignant if you suggested she was in any way psychic. She'd think it wasn't quite nice. The most that she would ever admit was that drawing people helped her to understand them."

"Quite." Sir Hubert nodded. "From the reports I read at the time, if my memory serves me, that is all her sketches showed, generally speaking; an acute understanding of human nature. Probably translations into her own medium of the impact of a personality rather than any manifestation of any latent psychic powers. No"—he overrode Delphick's attempt to speak—"that's a comment, not a criticism, so far. If Chief Superintendent Gosslin approves . . . ?" He looked at Delphick's immediate superior.

Gosslin hunched his bulk forward in his chair. "It's all a bit—well, I suppose you might say a bit above my head, sir. If a man's proved himself a good officer I think he should be allowed to follow his own line. Unless there's good reason against it. But feelings and fancies aren't my strong point and half the time I don't pretend to understand 'em. When it comes to drawing conclusions from evidence I know where I am and I think I'm as good as most. But when it comes to drawing pictures—from no evidence—well, that's just not up my street. But that's the point here. There is no evidence. In this particular selection of child killings we've got to admit we've nothing to go on worth a damn. Apart from knowing he must be cracked we're no further forward than when the first one happened. I've got to the pitch where any idea that might turn up something's worth thinking about. However farfetched."

"Even," mused the assistant commissioner, "so far as this gruesome idea of Delphick's to fetch an elderly and inoffensive lady to a mortuary, force her to look at a child's corpse and then expect her to make a sketch of it. In the hope, presumably, that the answer to his murder will be stamped all over his face, or thereabouts."

Damn, decided Delphick, that put paid to it. After the second killing, realizing that he was up against a nut case, he'd decided that he needed to study up on nuts and methods of cracking them. He'd weighed the advantages of consulting an alienist, but finally he had gone down to the small private nursing home outside Plummergen for an interview with Dr. Knight whom he had met and liked during Miss Seeton's escapades the previous summer. Before his retirement to the country for reasons of health, Dr. Knight had been London's leading neurologist. The doctor had been interested in Delphick's problem and interested in exposition, but, returning to London in a whirl of psychomotor epilepsy—which appeared to be what he had always thought of as schizophrenia—and schizophrenia, which apparently was not, Delphick had ruefully concluded that he would have done as well to continue into the village for a conference with Miss Seeton, who might have thrown in a drawing of the murderer for good measure. The idea had stuck. After the third and fourth killings the idea had become an obsession—a possible, a just barely possible, means of getting some clue to work on. And then this evening at Lewisham suddenly he'd been certain. Back in his office he'd tried to reason it out coldly and logically before consulting his chief and had only succeeded in convincing himself that it was the logical answer. But now—no. The A.C. was right. To think of dragging Miss Seeton in to make a drawing of a dead child she'd never even seen ... Granted last year, when she'd stopped being a public menace with her umbrella and taken up her pencil, she'd given him several clues to people and their doings, whether it was insight, intuition, thought transference or plain psychic, but they'd all been drawings of characters she'd seen, spoken to, or had dealings with. But just from a dead body—what could she be expected to get from that? In any case he hadn't thought enough of the effect on the old girl herself. She'd probably end up in hospital. And to have got the chief to set up this conference … Idiocy born of desperation. It would put a black mark against him with the A.C. Quite mad.

"Quite mad," pursued Sir Hubert. "Which, as we're all agreed that we're up against a madman, has, I suppose, a logic of its own. If other police forces can employ Croiset and his ilk, I see no reason why we should lag behind. Particularly if we have a home-grown product of our own—no expensive plane fares to account for—and even more particularly if we don't have to admit to what we're doing. We can employ her in the ordinary way, purely as an artist. I'll have a word with the receiver and arrange about a suitable fee. And expenses, within reason. Is she in London?"

Gosslin humphed. "No such luck. We got on to the school in Hampstead where she teaches but of course it's Easter and they said she's down in Kent. Some cottage she was left, Delphick knows it, in that little village where she got up to all those shenanigans last year."

Delphick realized that he must stop this before it went any further. "But after what you said, sir, I do see now …"

"Is the moment?" took up Sir Hubert. "I agree. You'd better get down there at once. Let's see, she's met your sergeant, hasn't she?"

Remembering, Delphick was forced to grin. "Yes, sir, but … "

The assistant commissioner became brisk. "You'd better take him with you then as driver; you'll need your wits about you when you arrive. Is there somewhere where you can stay?"

"Well, sir," it was getting out of hand, "last time we stayed at the George and Dragon, but I … "

"Book rooms there then, see Miss Seeton tonight and if you can persuade her bring her back with you in the morning." Sir Hubert opened a diary on his desk.

Delphick glanced at his chief for help, but Gosslin was looking elsewhere. "Excuse me, sir." He must be definite. "You, yourself…"

"Yes, yes, of course," interrupted Sir Hubert. He turned a page in the diary. "Now, let me see shall we say tomorrow at four o'clock? No, I may not be through by then. Better make it half past, if you think that will give her time enough. Will she want to do the drawing at the mortuary, do you know, or does she work from memory?"

"From memory I think mostly, sir. At least the sketches of hers I've seen have all been done that way."

The assistant commissioner nodded. "Well, I imagine you'll be kept busy at Lewisham during the early part of the afternoon, so you'd better leave her in charge of your sergeant. He can give her lunch and bring her back here; they can use your room. That won't worry or upset her, will it?"

In spite of himself, Delphick laughed. "I—er—shouldn't think so, sir. From what I remember of Miss Seeton, very little worries her. And the only thing that upset her was the newspaper publicity. She considered it vulgar. It'd be Sergeant Ranger who'd worry. She made him feel like Alice in Wonderland—a bit out of his depth."

"Right." Sir Hubert closed his diary and pushed it aside. "Then unless I hear from you to the contrary, we'll make it here at four-thirty tomorrow. I'll lay on tea. Your sergeant had better join the party. Unorthodox, but then the whole thing's unprecedented so we may as well keep it as informal as possible. Make her feel more at home," he surveyed his office, "or less far from it. Oh, yes, and one other thing," he continued as Delphick was about to speak. "I'd better know in advance your reason for getting Miss Seeton to sketch dead bodies instead of the normal procedure of employing a photographer. What excuse are you making to her—and, incidentally, to the Lewisham Division?"

Delphick's chance had come. "Personally I …"

"Excellent," cut in Sir Huburt. "Personality. Yes, that should hold water, or nearly. Even the cleverest photographs of dead bodies are no more than just that. If the eyes are closed they look dead and if the eyes are open they look as if they belonged on a fishmonger's slab. No personality whatever."

Desperate, Delphick stood up. "Sir—"

"Yes?"

"Listening to you earlier on—"

"You flatter me," broke in Sir Hubert. "I'd no idea people did. I thought they just let me ramble on while paying no attention, or very little."

Delphick refused to be deflected. "You said that my idea was mad."

"I did," agreed the assistant commissioner. "And had you been listening as closely as you suggest you would have noted that I added that that very madness carried a possible advantage."

Delphick stuck with it. "But you see, sir, I hadn't considered…"

Sir Hubert raised a hand. He looked astonished. "Not considered? My dear Superintendent, I hope you're not trying to tell me at this stage that this whole concept of yours was some impulsive whim. That you had not considered what you were doing when you consulted Chief Superintendent Gosslin. That you had not considered what you were doing when, being a question of finance as well as policy, the buck was passed to me and the chief superintendent arranged this meeting, at a moment's notice, keeping me overtime, for which, incidentally, I'm not paid, so that I might listen to your proposal and allow myself to be persuaded by your arguments. I do hope, Superintendent, that you're not now trying to tell me that none of this was considered. That it was just a passing caprice."

"No, sir, of course not. I …"

"Of course not. I apologize for the thought. Such a lack of consideration would have been," he measured his words, "quite inexcusable. And now, get off to Kent at once or your Miss Seeton will have gone to bed before you get there." Sir Hubert nodded dismissal, took a file from his desk, opened it, and began to read.

Dazed, Delphick left.

Gosslin harrumphed. "I kept out of it, sir, but you don't think you were a bit hard on the Oracle, shoving him along like that? He was beginning to get cold feet about this way-out notion of his."

"Beginning?" Sir Hubert dropped his file back on his desk. "I should've called it advanced frostbite. But he hadn't, you know, considered it, not from this woman's angle. And I thought he should. This case is getting on top of him. After that, if I hadn't administered a gentle shove, to borrow from your elegance in phraseology, it would have ended with my being forced to adopt his brainchild myself and order him to carry it out. Which wouldn't have suited me, or not as well."

"You mean," Gosslin blew out his cheeks, "you go for all this psychic stuff? You think this Seeton woman'll really cough up something? You believe in it?"

"Do I?" The assistant commissioner was thoughtful. "No, I can't say I do, or very little. No, my motives were quite other, or largely. Judging from the police and press reports of her adventures last year, I should say that the woman is undoubtedly a catalyst." His eyes flickered to Gosslin.

The chief superintendent grinned. "Something that changes metals, sir."

"Well, yes," acknowledged Sir Hubert. "Generally speaking it does that, of course. But the dictionary definition is 'a substance which, added to other substances, facilitates a chemical reaction in which it is, itself, not consumed.' The case of these child killings is at a standstill on our side. It needs a change, or change of approach. By dropping a catalyst into it I'm hoping to get a reaction. In other words, although Miss Seeton may, almost certainly will, remain the same, the case, more than likely, will not."

The car forked left in Brettenden. On seeing the sign, Plummergen Road, Sergeant Ranger had a thought.

"Sir?"

"M'm?"

"You know what that village is like and how they natter. And they always get hold of the wrong end of the stick. If we stay overnight at the pub and then take Miss Seeton away with us in the morning, half the place will probably think she's been arrested."

"Damn," said Delphick, "I hadn't thought of that."

Chapter 2

"If you ask me, she's been arrested. And a pound of apples, please."

In a city a local newspaper will keep the public abreast of locational affairs from day to day. In a village such a publication would be uneconomic, but public-spirited persons will always be found to shoulder the burden and to relay news items of parochial interest from hour to hour.

In Plummergen the undisputed directors of this voluntary broadcasting system are a Miss Erica Nuttel and a Mrs. Norah—Bunny to her friend—Blaine, vegetarian ladies, known as the Nuts. The house which they share, inevitably the Nut House, although the name on the gate reads "Lilikot," has large plate-glass windows, and is the most modern of the patchwork of styles and periods which line the Street. Since Plummergen has only the one street, Lilikot's situation in the centre of it, opposite Crabbe's garage, ensures that there is little that the two ladies miss, if much they misinterpret, of the comings and goings of the inhabitants.

Perhaps the quickest and most satisfying method of spreading news is to go shopping. Plummergen has five shops: a tiny bakery, a small butcher's, and three rival stores: the grocer's, the draper's, and the post office. Of these last the post office has become the most important: more up-to-date than its competitors, with a wider range of groceries than the grocer, a more comprehensive selection of clothes than the draper, and three deep freezers instead of one.

"Arrested? Of course, Eric, you're too right," agreed Norah Blaine. She picked up a tin of mock meatballs and studied the colorful imagery on the wrapper: brown spheres flecked with green mildew, floating on crimson lake. "It's too obvious what's happened and it doesn't surprise me in the least. It's only what I've said all along. I mean people don't get mixed up in murders and things unless there's more in it than meets the eye. Well, I mean, do they?"

Unfortunately for her, Miss Seeton had. Before her arrival the previous summer after the death of Mrs. Bannet, her godmother and only relative, to assess her inheritance of a cottage and a diminutive income, Miss Seeton had had the mischance to be the sole witness of a murder in London and the ramifications of the case, which had followed her down to Kent, had been treated by the villagers as a rare show put on for their entertainment.

Miss Nuttel pronounced judgment. "Shouldn't've thought so. Don't get mixed up in murders myself."

"Exactly," triumphed Mrs. Blaine. "That proves it. After all, she's only been back here two or three days. School holidays indeed." She tittered. "More likely to be …"

"Running away?" suggested Miss Nuttel.

"Well, naturally, we don't know anything. And I would be the last to make any accusation. But it's too clear what's happened. The police in London must have found out something, so she's come back here to get away and they've followed her down and arrested her. And high time too in my opinion after what happened yesterday. Knocking little Effie Goffer down in the middle of the road and nearly getting her run over. And the car drove straight on without stopping. These hit-and-run drivers are too careless, it shouldn't be allowed. And Miss Seeton ought to be ashamed of herself."

A ripple of excitement shimmered through other shoppers in the post office, who had unobtrusively drifted close in order to miss no revelation from that prime minister of the gossip according to Mrs. Blaine, in her new testament, unauthorized and abridged. The leader of the opposition had arrived and was standing only a few feet behind Miss Nuttel and her friend. It was known that Miss Treeves frowned on scandalmongering.

"Good morning, Miss Nuttel. Good morning, Mrs. Blaine."

Norah Blaine started and nearly dropped the tin. The audience held a collective breath. Mrs. Blaine turned to smile at the vicar's sister and decided that a frontal attack would be her best gambit.

"Oh, good morning, Miss Treeves, perhaps you could tell us. We were just wondering …"

"About Miss Seeton?" The tone was censorious. "So I heard."

"Well, it does seem too …"

"Odd," supplied Miss Nuttel.

The postmaster, returning with the apples weighed and bagged, contributed a diversion. "Was there anything else?"

Miss Nuttel frowned. "Don't think so. Anything more you wanted, Bunny?"

"Well, these—" Mrs. Blaine held out the tin of mock meatballs. "Of course, as you know, we never touch meat—what are these made of?"

As a shopkeeper, Mr. Stillman approved the little that he had seen of Miss Seeton. A very pleasant, ordinary little body, with nice manners, thoughtful, and paid her account on the dot, which was more than you could say of some. He gave the two ladies a bland look.

"Nuts," said Mr. Stillman.

The collective breath was released in a sigh of enjoyment.

Unaware of their nickname, Mrs. Blaine decided: "We'll take them then." She collected their purchases, put them into her shopping bag, and moved from the counter to face Miss Treeves. "But you must admit the whole thing does seem too odd, doesn't it?" she continued. "We did just happen to see you call at Miss Seeton's cottage this morning at about half past nine, when I was leaning out of the window, dusting—that was after the police had come for her, of course. . . ."

"So perhaps you don't know any more than we do," suggested Miss Nuttel.

"As it happens, I do." Miss Treeves wished she did. Anyway, lying in a good cause wasn't lying at all, simply—well, justifiable invention. "The superintendent from Scotland Yard wanted Miss Seeton's help," she improvised.

"Exactly what we were saying," agreed Mrs. Blaine.

"Helping the police with their inquiries," concluded Miss Nuttel.

By village standards the motion of censure had failed, but a gain had been made by the independent Mr. Stillman. With winning smiles the two ladies bowed and left the shop to continue their mission across the Street.

The simplifications of life in the country are evident and easy to understand. To take an example; it is impossible to get lost in a village with only one street. In compensation, however, the roads leading into Plummergen from the north, through Brettenden or via Ashford, are not easy and the way out of the village is difficult to find. The Street itself, straight, wide, and tree-lined, runs direct from north to south where, at first glance, it would appear to stop. Beyond the gravel sweep outside the George and Dragon a left turn leads into the churchyard. On the opposite side of the Street there is a right-hand turn, Marsh Road, concealed behind the garden next door to the bakery. It is signposted Rye, no distance specified; a fantasy on the part of the local council which is appreciated only by the immediate neighborhood. Although it is possible, with map or compass, to escape its serpentine curves and to reach Rye by a series of intertwined lanes, Marsh Road is, in effect, what it says: a road round the other side of the marsh which leads back to Brettenden. For those wishing to depart from Plummergen southward, the Street does, in fact, continue as a narrow lane sandwiched between the side wall which bounds Miss Seeton's garden and the house next door. After some twenty yards the lane relents and widens for the bridge over the canal. On the immediate right of this is the only direct route to Rye, a hidden turning, unposted and unmarked on any map, save as the canal beside which it runs. Beyond this turning the road ends in a T junction, both arms of which meander toward the coast road, Folkestone to the left, Hastings to the right. In practice these southern roads are little used by the villagers. Although Rye, over five miles away, is the nearest town, for business or for pleasure Plummergen goes north to Brettenden, six miles, or even more than double that distance into Ashford. There is a daily bus service to both these towns. There is no bus to Rye. There is no local bus service south of Plummergen. This curious fact stems perhaps from distrust: distrust of modern ways and new inventions. Rye, that upstart little island which became a Norman port, ranks as a modern invention and the way to it is new. In the days when Plummergen flourished as a Roman port the land to the south of the present village was still but a deep-sea dream.

Her shopping completed, Miss Treeves headed for the vicarage, which stood back between the George and Dragon and the churchyard, to prepare her brother's lunch. On the other side of the Street she noticed Mrs. Blaine and Miss Nuttel leave Welsted's, the draper's, and turn in at the gate of Lilikot.

She must find out, Miss Treeves decided, exactly what this business with the police was all about and see to it that it was spread round the village so that it was clearly understood. It would bc such a shame if this holiday was spoiled for Miss Seeton. How tiresome people were, inventing stupid stories and then believing them, never thinking of the trouble and unpleasantness they caused, instead of waiting to find out the truth, which was usually dull. Of course it might be to do with old Mrs. Bannet's solicitor, wretched man, who'd gone to prison for embezzlement and, she believed, something to do with drugs. Making them or selling them—or something. In fact, if she remembered rightly, the police had arrested him before Miss Seeton's probate had finally been granted. But naturally—how simple—that would be it. Some extra information that the police needed in clearing up the mess that that horrible man had left behind. What a pity that she hadn't realized it while she was in the post office.

By the time Miss Treeves reached the vicarage gate this simple, natural explanation had become fact in her mind. She gave Miss Seeton's cottage a glance of satisfaction. Before the owner returned, she would see to it that everything was made quite clear and the truth known. The front door of Sweetbriars, one of the short row of houses that faced down the Street, opened and Martha Bloomer appeared.

Miss Seeton's legacy from her godmother had included the latter's arrangement with a local farmhand and his wife. Miss Seeton providing the requirements, Stan Bloomer looked after the garden and the hen houses, supplying Miss Seeton and his own family with eggs, chickens and vegetables, and selling the surplus for his personal profit instead of wages, while his wife Martha came to help in the house two mornings a week for three and sixpence an hour.

Mrs. Bloomer closed the door of the cottage and started down the path to the gate. Suddenly she pounced sideways at the hedge inside the wooden paling, to reappear dragging a protesting and disheveled little girl. Martha Bloomer—the very person. Miss Treeves dropped the latch of the vicarage gate and crossed the Street.

"You let me catch you snooping round here again, you nasty little sneak, and I'll give you a thundering good walloping and what's more I'm going to speak to your mum," warned Mrs. Bloomer.

Effie Goffer sniffed.

"Effie," admonished Miss Treeves as she joined them, "how dare you pry about in other people's gardens like that? You've been spoken to about it before. What were you doing?"

"Watchin'."

"Well, don't let me catch you at it again or I'll see you're given a good spanking. Miss Wicks was complaining about you only the other day."

Effie's eyes gleamed. "She tikes ter bits."

"Rubbish."

"Doesan'all.Watched'erthrough'erbathroomwindyan'she tikesterbits.Took'erteethoutan'put'emintheglass.Took'er'air too an' stuck it on the shelf. Saw 'er."

Miss Treeves was outraged. "Effie, how can you speak like that? How dare you repeat such dreadful things?" The more dreadful in that they were true. Miss Wicks's squirrel teeth which made her hiss so when she spoke—surely her dentist could have … And of course the false piece she wore was obvious because the color was wrong. But it didn't do to say so. It was possible to ignore such things provided they weren't spoken of. But, once discussed, they assumed a hypnotic quality which kept you mesmerized, with the danger, when you were talking to Miss Wicks, of patting your own hair or, worse, hissing back.

"The lidy's doin' me picture. Modeled for 'er I did so I's watchin'!" whined Effie.

"Nonsense," replied Miss Treeves. "In any case, Miss Seeton isn't here at the moment."

"No," agreed Effie, "cos the police took 'er. Saw 'em."

"You saw them?"

"Iss. Same ones as was down 'ere before. The tecs from Lunnon." Hurt her bum the old cow had, knocking her down like that with her brolly. She'd teach her to hurt her bum. " 'Andcuffed she was just like on teevee an' she were kickin' an' screamin' …"

Martha Bloomer shook her. "Why, you little liar—"

"Effie," cut in Miss Treeves, "go home at once. And tell your mother," she added ominously, "that I shall be in to see her after lunch."

Miss Treeves watched the toadlike figure stump its way the length of the Street toward the council houses at the far end. She shook her head. "That child'll come to a bad end."

"If you ask me," snapped Mrs. Bloomer, "she's bad already and the end can't come too soon. Handcuffs indeed, how dare she? And screaming. I'd give her screaming if I'd anything to do with her."

"You didn't happen to see Miss Seeton yourself before she left?"

"Well, no, you see I wouldn't today being one of my mornings at the Hall. But I looked in, case she'd left a message which she didn't not expecting, and I found some overs in the fridge so I made her a hotchpotch pie because I doubt she'll be tired when she gets back and it'll do for her supper tonight or her lunch tomorrow according."

"She'll stay the night at her flat," decided Miss Treeves. "Less wearing. She's not giving it up till the end of next term when she retires and settles down here permanently."

This arbitrary posting was less certain than Miss Treeves supposed. Miss Seeton's pleasure in her inheritance and her growing love for the cottage were tempered by a financial problem; if she did indeed retire at the end of the next school term, would the tiny income, added to her small savings and her old-age pension, prove sufficient? To live in the country would entail giving up her classes at the Polytechnic, though these, of course, were now becoming Evening Institutes, and her few private pupils, the pay from whom had helped to eke out her salary for her twice weekly attendance at the school.

Against that there would be no rent and her expenses on food would be less; but there would be such items as maintenance and repairs to consider. Then, too, there would be rates which, in Miss Seeton's experience, had a strange way of going up, whereas the value of money had an equally curious disposition to go down.

"It would be nice for you, too, Martha," continued Miss Treeves, "having looked after old Mrs. Bannet for years, to feel that the cottage is staying in the family."

"I should hope so," agreed Martha. "And you say she won't be back till tomorrow?"

Miss Treeves glanced over at the vicarage. She'd be late with Arthur's lunch. Not that he'd ever notice, but still. "I'm not certain," she said quickly, "it all depends how long this business about her solicitor takes."

"Her solicitor?" Martha was surprised. "But I thought that was all over and done with. He's over and done with, too. He's in quod."

Miss Treeves became impatient. "Yes, yes, of course he is. But it's something to do with those people he defrauded—I don't know the ins and outs of it—but the police are hoping Miss Seeton can give them some information."

"Well, you do surprise me. She hardly knew him and didn't like him neither. Those detectives were always interested in her pictures and I'd made sure they'd come down to ask her to do some Identikit drawings for them."

Miss Treeves dismissed the idea. "No, no, nothing like that. It's to do with the embezzlement case. And now I really must fly or lunch'll never be ready." She turned to go, looked back. "Oh, and, Martha, Miss Nuttel and Mrs. Blaine were talking earlier—and rather stupidly—so if anyone asks,

I think it would be as well if you mentioned the embezzlement business so that it's quite clear. It's important to get the truth established as soon as possible because if that dreadful Effie Goffer starts spreading stories around, heaven knows what everybody will be saying."

"They'll say anything." Lady Colveden poured herself another cup of tea. "Anything at all."

Life in a small community has a mystique to bewilder the metropolitan. In a city, failing some act which leads to notoriety, the individual will be ignored. In a village everyone's actions, notorious or not, are of interest to the commonalty and are subject to the same scrutiny and detailed analysis.

At the beginning of Marsh Road the houses are all set well back, all have drives, all are tree-screened. To the urbanite they would appear to be, in the literal sense, private houses. Privacy, however, which is taken for granted in the metropolis, does not exist in the small community.

Recently Major General Sir George Colveden, Bart., K.C.B., D.S.O., J.P., owner of the last estate in Marsh Road, had found his nearest neighbor, a widow in her sixties, swinging an amateur ax at a cypress in his grounds. Balked, the lady complained to the Brettenden Rural District Council. By lending her late husband's binoculars to the district surveyor she proved to her satisfaction, if not to his, that her complaint was justified. Owing to the tree's growth, her view had been ruined: she could no long see the bedroom windows at Rytham Hall; in consequence she had now no idea at what time Lady Colveden turned out her light nor when she drew her curtains in the morning. For some days Lady Colveden had found herself glancing nervously skyward, lest the lady should have taken to a tethered balloon or a helicopter in an attempt to satisfy her very natural curiosity about her neighbors' private affairs.

"I told Martha this morning," Lady Colveden eyed the empty cake plate, "that if she took time off from cleaning to make doughnuts you'd overeat, Nigel. Where do you put it all? If I eat one I bulge. But you wolf down three and nothing shows. It's not fair. Absolutely anything," she reverted.

"A hard-working thyroid and hard work," her son informed her. "We sowed the Fouracre this afternoon, including half an hour wasted on taking the tractor to bits when the engine played up. Anything," he queried. "Ah, for instance?"

"About poor Miss Seeton, of course. Have you ever heard anything so ridiculous? And, anyway, I don't consider that hard work—riding around in a tractor. I can remember when a man walked round with a horse."

"You can't, you know."

"Well, I've read about it which comes to exactly the same thing and they tasted much better."

"The man or the horse?"

"Don't be vulgar. But it seems so unfair. The poor little thing's only been down here a couple of days. And now this. It was bad enough last year. But if this sort of thing's going to happen every time she comes here …"

"Not every time, mother. After all, she was down here at Christmas and nothing happened to her then."

Wide, innocent eyes gazed at him in surprise. "At Christmas? How do you know? We shouldn't've noticed anyway, that was during the war."

War had been declared on Christmas Eve.

Miss Nuttel, Mrs. Blaine, and three of their cronies had spent the summer drying flowers, foliage, and grasses.

Bunches of wilt and wither had festooned their kitchens, striking their guardians in the face at every turn and flavoring the cooking. In the morning on Christmas Eve they had carried this decayed vegetation in triumph to the church, where they had spent a satisfying hour arranging it in the vases and, after a proud look around, had left in the knowledge of a deed well done.

During the afternoon Lady Colveden, as one of the committee, arrived to decorate the Christmas tree. Shocked to find the church filled with the remains of dead flowers, she had emptied the vases, thrown the lot out, and burned them. She had driven home to Rytham Hall and cut some Lenten roses, which flower in December as opposed to Christmas roses which rarely bloom before Lent, and after two hours of hard work, the tree and the floral decorations completed, she had given a quick look round and left in the knowledge of a good deed done.

In the resulting brouhaha the village had divided into two camps. Words had been exchanged, smiles had been hurled, and parting shots had been fired at the end of meetings. The uncivil strife had raged unabated until February, when an uneasy armistice had been imposed by a very sharp letter in the parish magazine signed by the Reverend Arthur, but rightly attributed to that more forceful character, his sister, Miss Treeves. The affair had duly been noted in parish history as the War of the Roses.

Nigel began to tabulate on his fingers. "Let's see. The first time Miss Seeton stayed at the cottage we were involved in murder, suicide, drowning, gas, shooting, car crashes, abduction, and embezzlement." He eyed his mother quizzically. "You think bickering about throwing away some dead flowers more important than that little lot."

"Naturally," replied Lady Colveden. "So would you if you'd done the throwing." There was a slight rustle of paper on the opposite side of the tea table as a tremor shook the hands that held the *Farmer's Breeding Weekly*. She addressed the newspaper. "George."

"Yes, m'dear."

"You're not paying attention."

"No, m'dear."

"Well, there you are," said Lady Colveden. "Of course it's Molly Treeves that shocks me. I'd believe anything of the rest of them, but I really should've thought Molly'd've had more sense."

Nigel finished his last doughnut, put down his plate, and wiped his fingers. "More sense than what?"

His mother stared at him in astonishment. "To repeat such an idiotic story, of course."

Her son restrained himself. "What story, mother? You forget that we farming types, lazing about the fields all day in our tractors, are apt to get out of touch."

"That Miss Seeton's been arrested for embezzlement."

"She's what?" cried Nigel. Sir George lowered his newspaper.

"There. You see," exclaimed Lady Colveden with satisfaction. "That's even got your father out of the pigsty. I was in Welsted's this afternoon and Mrs. Welsted told me that the Nuts had told her that that horrible little Effie Goffer had actually seen them take her away—that nice detective from Scotland Yard and that huge young man with the notebook who's fallen for Anne Knight, I can't remember his name, the older one I mean, foreign or something."

"Superintendent Delphick?" asked Nigel.

"That's right, Greek …" She broke off. "George, why are you staring at me like that?"

"Paying attention, m'dear."

"Well, don't. I'm not used to it and it's very unnerving. I think it must have been Effie who started it. I can't imagine why somebody hasn't done something about that child with all this 'I Spy' business of hers."

"That one needs strangling," agreed Nigel.

"Oh, don't," protested his mother. "There was another in the papers only this morning. A little boy at Lewisham. I do wish they wouldn't. But if they must strangle children, I do admit we could spare Effie. Should we advertise or something?"

"Stick to the point, mother, and don't rattle."

Lady Colveden was hurt. "As if my big end'd gone. Well, I told Mrs. Welsted it was complete nonsense, but she assured me that someone else had been in who'd got it from Martha, who'd got it from Molly Treeves, that it was embezzlement. Really, people. Anyway, that's quite ridiculous, because it was Martha's day here this morning and she never mentioned it then." She pondered, then brightened. "Actually, in some ways I think it'll be a very good thing if Miss Seeton starts up again."

"Starts what?" asked Nigel.

"Oh," his mother looked round the room for inspiration, "murders and things. I don't think she can help it. I think she's one of those people things happen to—or she happens to them, I'm not sure which—without her noticing it. It'll give the village lots to talk about and then perhaps at last they'll forget those wretched flowers."

"Embezzlement story's got to be stopped," remarked Sir George.

"Oh, it has been," his wife assured him. "I stopped it. I told Mrs. Welsted that Miss Seeton was dining here tonight."

"Here?" ejaculated Nigel.

"Yes. I called at Crabbe's garage and found out that Scotland Yard had ordered a car to meet Miss Seeton at Headcorn on the six-forty, so I canceled the car and told him not to go."

"You ...?" For once Nigel was speechless.

"Yes. I thought you could go and fetch her while I get on with the dinner. And drive rather slowly down the Street on the way back so that everyone can see. And I decided if the poor little thing's tired, I'll make her put her feet up on the sofa and give her dinner on a tray."

"You—you mean," spluttered Nigel, "that you're going to hijack her just to find out what she's been up to?"

"Not at all," retorted his mother. "It's just a kindness. It'll help to put a stop to the talk. And, anyway, it'll be one in the eye for the Nuts. And if she chooses to tell us what she's been doing, there's no harm in listening, is there? Actually I explained the whole thing to Mrs. Welsted—and to Crabbe—so it should've got around by now. I told them that she'd gone up to London because Scotland Yard had engaged her to do some drawings for them. There's not a word of truth in it, of course, but I thought it better than the other story."

Sir George's eyes bulged. "Happens to be true."

"Oh, don't be silly, George!" exclaimed his wife. "You're not listening. Of course it isn't true. I just told you. I made it up on the spur of the moment."

"True," insisted Sir George. "Delphick rang me this morning to explain, before leaving."

"Oh, really, George!" She was exasperated. "You're quite impossible. Do you mean to sit there and tell me that you've known this all along and never said a word?"

"Not our business."

"Of course it is. Everybody makes it their business, and it's our business to protect her. And there have I been running round the village inventing lies with the best of intentions, when all the time, if you'd only told me, I could perfectly well have invented the truth."

While in a narrow sense the quirks of the countryside may be difficult for the city-bred to grasp, on a wider scope the over-all picture is easier to realize from afar. From London distance can give perspective to the view; if it does not lend enchantment.

"Rats, you just can't do this to me. I'd die—just die."

"I'll send a wreath," promised the editor of the *Daily Negative*. "On expense account."

"But," Amelita Forby gripped the edge of the editor's desk with both hands and leaned forward, "goddammit, this is Fleet Street—the Street. This is my home town." She snatched a pencil from his desk; prodded his arm. "Remember me? I'm the one you said could go Crime—not Foreign Correspondent. I'm a city girl. What do yu expect me to do in some Godforsaken dump?"

The editor tilted his chair beyond the range of the jabbing pencil. "Gain experience and widen your horizon."

Miss Forby snorted. "My first week in this setup widened my horizon to a fifty-foot screen. And as for experience … Boy—more loss than gain. Anyway, where is this damn Plum-whatever? How do I get there? Do I need a passport?"

"I don't think so," said the editor reasonably. "It's listed as a British possession. You could always go on safari to Ashford and then write Plummergen on a piece of paper and show it around till someone says 'Aye' or 'Ah' or whatever they say down there. You should be grateful for the assignment, Mel. Think of it. March, with spring just round the corner. Kent's known as the garden of England. And they say it's very bracing." He shuddered.

"Bracing, for God's sake." She flung down the pencil. "And do I look like a garden flower?"

He studied her angry face. "Frankly, no. More like an overheated orchid." He dropped his chair back and pushed the pencil out of her reach. "Sorry, Mel, but it's all yours. My spies tell me that Delphick fetched her up to London, took her to Lewisham this morning, and now they've gone on to the Yard. I want to know why." He grinned at his irate subordinate. "You'll go down there and you'll stay down there till you've got the story."

"And if nothing happens?"

"Then you'd better marry a farmer and settle down. I don't want to see you back in the office till this one's wrapped up." He spoke slowly, thoughtful: "I've got a feeling about it—got a nose for these things. Lewisham. Where that kid was strangled yesterday. Mel," he was suddenly enthusiastic, "this could be one of the big ones. And at least on this Seeton woman's previous form, you should have a lively time."

"Previous form?" she exploded. "For Pete's sake, I read all about her previous form last year. The Battling Brolly. Some overmuscled battle-ax of a schoolmarm busting her way through life with an umbrella. You know just what you can do with your feelings. And you can do the same with your nose."

The editor shook his head. "In my opinion that business last year was badly handled in the press. I think it needs a woman's touch."

"You do? Well, in my opinion, it's you who're touched. From what I remember reading, it would need an all-inwrestler to handle her." She pushed back her chair and stood up. "I'd better get myself a workout at a gym someplace."

The editor clasped his hands on the desk and spoke seriously. "Listen, Mel. You don't stay in newspapers as long as I have without learning to smell when something's cooking. I'm giving you a free hand. Handle it anyway you like. Slant it anyway you want. But stay with it till you've got it. You're in on it from the beginning—before it's begun even. So make it a story and make it good. Deliver once, twice, three times a week, or daily—depending how it pans out. I'm leaving instructions for your copy not to be spiked, so don't overwrite—or spend."

"Not spiked?" She gaped at him. "You must've flipped. And what d'you mean—you're leaving?"

"I'm leaving tomorrow morning for Italy. And a fortnight's sun—I hope."

Mel Forby stopped in the doorway. "See Naples—" she suggested venomously, "and I'll stand your wreath myself." The door slammed.

The editor chuckled. He pulled forward an internal phone.

"Dick? I've told Mel—she's madder'n a hatter, but as she'll be quitting town tonight you won't have to cope. Leave her alone down there and print whatever she sends in just as is." He listened for a moment. "Of course it'll be God-awful, that's what I want, and don't let others catch on to why she's there. If anyone's interested it's a sob-sister rehash on the Battling Brolly settling down quietly to live a quiet life in the quiet countryside. And the quieter it's kept the better I'll like it." The telephone protested. "You don't have to worry," the editor told it. "It's a calculated risk, and the calculation and the risk're both mine. I've cleared it upstairs so you've got no comeback coming and anyway Mel doing maybe-crime reporting in a village and a temper should be good for a laugh. Personally I'll take a bet it'll pan out—might become a popular feature." He put back the receiver and laughed to himself. Pity to be away and miss it. Mel on Fashion was one thing, but Mel as a crime correspondent should be out of this world. But she'd get the facts if there were any and no rival was likely to cotton to it and start sending its own men down to muscle in. If he was right in what he thought was hatching, the *Negative* was going to get a scoop.

Chapter 3

Miss Seeton's sketch lay upon the assistant commissioner's desk.

Curious, reflected Sir Hubert, to have such a feeling of disappointment. He hadn't expected much, if anything at all, but the feeling of let-down persisted.

Delphick, too, felt depressed. It had been a chance. And the chance hadn't come off. But it wasn't until now that he recognized how high his hopes had been. He had ridden roughshod over Miss Seeton's objections last night. And she had objected; had proved, for her, curiously stubborn. He had appealed to her, pleaded with her, and finally, when it had dawned on him that it was not that she was loath to visit a mortuary but, which seemed strange, that she was unwilling to do any drawing at all, he had resorted to moral bullying before she would consent. In view of the result, perhaps she'd been right. He should have left well alone.

Waste of time. Chief Superintendent Gosslin shifted in his chair and tried to think of an excuse to get back to his office and get on with some work. The Oracle had slipped up on this one. If that was art, give him photos, front and side, any day. Looked as if she'd started all right, got bored, and then, realizing what a duff she was making, crossed it all out and done a bit of geometry.

The assistant commissioner, lifting the teapot, glanced at the drawing again. The left side of the face wasn't bad, probably quite a recognizable likeness though a bit blurred, but the right side was a mess; smudged, unfinished, and in some way repellent. Then why those regular wavy lines drawn across it with, after a break, two half circles, one within the other? Useless. But, looking at it again, the sketch had an undeniable—a haunting—quality. You couldn't dismiss it; nor forget it. He pulled himself together and made a determined social effort.

"Tell me, Miss Seeton," Sir Hubert handed her a second cup of tea, "these character drawings of yours or perhaps, more correctly, I should say these cartoons, of which the superintendent has been telling me, have you always done them? Or are they a recent development?"

How very awkward. She could wish Sir Hubert hadn't asked her that. She sipped her tea—so very strong. But no sugar, thank goodness. Miss Seeton's dilemma was real. She knew that she must give a truthful reply and yet the truth was difficult to define. Cartoons? Character drawings? She had never thought of them as such. And had she always done them? That again was difficult to answer.

She had in fact always done such drawings but she had learned to frown upon the doing. It was her early aptitude for revealing sketches of people and events from memory that had led her to take up art as a profession. It would be easy to imagine that two fairy godmothers had attended at Miss Seeton's christening, each determined to do her best for the child according to her lights, but without previous consultation. The first, in the grand convention, diaphanously garbed and with a glittering wand, had waved that wand and had ordained: This child shall be a Great Original; adventures shall befall her; danger shall be her portion; but she shall always triumph in adversity and shall stand as an example of how Right shall vanquish Wrong. The second godmother, in a more modern convention, tweed coat and skirt and with an umbrella in her hand, had raised that umbrella and decreed: This child shall be meek; full of humility and grace; she shall conform to an accepted pattern; she shall prove the triumph of Respectability over Disorder in this world. Both ladies might then have taken off in individual puffs of smoke, congratulating themselves on their good intentions, unaware that between them they had set their little godchild the unenviable task of treading two divergent paths through life. It is a credit to Miss Seeton's character that she has so far kept one foot on each of these split ways without doing in actual fact the splits. At art school Miss Seeton's ebullience of pencil and her lightning sketches met with disapproval. That great cartoonist of the century's turn Phil May, it was explained, had always worked in meticulous detail before choosing the few brief lines that he would oversketch in ink. No one but genius, it was pointed out, should attempt to work freehand and only then after long and arduous study. Miss Seeton's humility could not envisage genius save in others. The meticulous and the arduous became her aim and the teaching of drawing to indifferent children her lot. Her occasional and irrepressible breakthroughs of inspiration and originality she deplored, or excused as being notes to be worked on later. So in her life Adventure sought her out, cavorted round her, and intruded. Miss Seeton, armored in Respectability, ignored it, or when perforce involved she used the Nelson Touch; refused to see that continual implication in strange circumstances implied a personal implication. In life, for her congenital imbroglios and escapades—such as prodding a young man in the back with her umbrella when he was in the act of striking a girl, with a view to reproving his manners, only to find that she had committed the solecism of intruding on a purely personal matter of murder—she would blame herself; a misconception here; there a failure to understand; nor would she admit to any sequence in such events since to do so would be to deny the placid, conventional existence she truly believed she led.

Equally, in work, any strangeness such as her recent difficulty in drawing could not, she was convinced, be due to an outside influence, but must, she was quite sure, have a mundane source—oneself—one's age. But she couldn't—no, she really couldn't go into all that. She'd known that to attempt any drawing just at the moment was unwise. But then the superintendent—such a kind, such an understanding man, as a rule—had been so persuasive, so insistent even. But, of course, she'd been wrong to agree, because it had been even worse this time. So very embarrassing. For everybody. However, it was no good worrying over what was done and couldn't be helped. And, in any case, she had an appointment with Dr. Knight tomorrow morning, so then, at least, she'd know where she stood. Meanwhile Sir Hubert's question was such a difficult one to answer. Truthfully, that was. And with the police, of course, it was so very important to be exact.

"I've always been inclined to do them," she confessed. "Though very seldom. And I've never approved. You see, I feel, as I've always tried to impress upon my pupils, that one should only draw precisely what one sees. Or as near as one can, that is. Imaginative work should only be for the highly trained. Or, of course, again, for the very gifted. And in either of these cases, naturally, the rules shouldn't apply. And, recognizing this tendency toward extravagance in myself, I've always tried to suppress it. Though I'm bound to admit that it does seem to have been getting worse since I've been standing on my head."

Gosslin wuffed; then retrieved to a cough when it dawned that he'd wuffed out of season. Too late he put his cup and saucer on the assistant commissioner's desk.

Sergeant Ranger had effaced himself so far as was possible by placing his chair against the wall, his notebook and pen on his knees, for confidence, teacup and saucer in one hand and a plate with a buttered bun in the other. He felt bitter. It should be even chances, but it never was. It was always odds on they fell buttered side down. He recovered his now bewhiskered bun and pushed the plate under his chair and out of his mind. Anyway, he hadn't poured tea all over his pants like old Goosefeathers.

Miss Seeton regarded Sir Hubert anxiously. "Of course," she continued, "I don't say there is necessarily any connection."

The assistant commissioner made a valiant effort. "No. I can see that you wouldn't say that. Or, not necessarily. But I quite appreciate that you feel bound to give consideration to the fact that the possibility is there. Or thereabouts." He looked helplessly at Delphick.

Delphick laughed. "So you're discovered; your secret is out. What made you take up yoga?"

"My knees," she explained. "The advertisement was so very encouraging that it seemed to be worth the attempt."

"Somehow, Miss Seeton," observed the assistant commissioner, "I find it difficult to picture you indulging in meditation or flights of fancy. Your feet—or more properly I should say your head—appear to be planted too firmly on the ground."

"Oh, no," Miss Seeton assured him. "I don't try anything mental. I believe it's very difficult and takes years."

"A pity," remarked Sir Hubert. "We could do with some mental gymnastics. The man we're looking for on this child murder case is certainly mental, or at best indifferent sane. Presuming always that it is only one man."

"You mean …?" Miss Seeton was shocked. "Oh, but surely, there couldn't be more than one?"

"We trust not. But a case that is given detailed coverage in the press is liable to produce imitative crimes. And in this instance the method is easy enough to copy. To cross your hands, to throw a loop of wire over your victim's head from behind, to jerk it tight, rendering him helpless, doesn't take any strength, or very little. A woman, even a child, could do it."

"I see." Miss Seeton frowned. "I hadn't thought of it in those terms. So you're looking for someone who's not strong. In a way—although still, of course, quite dreadful—it does make it more understandable."

"Why?" rapped Delphick.

"Why? But—but, as Sir Hubert said, because it explains why children."

"Why children?" echoed the assistant commissioner.

For a moment she was puzzled. "I do see that with someone weak—and perhaps small—trying to … well, I suppose you could call it to prove themselves—make themselves important—that they'd have to, presumably, attack someone smaller than themselves, as you said."

"Thank you, Miss Seeton." Sir Hubert smiled. "I didn't. But you have." It was a slant, a shift in emphasis that might give them a new approach. The Oracle was on to it. This comic little character had more plain horse sense than many. She could certainly outride all those trick cyclists who'd been writing in the papers. They'd given her quite a day one way and another. Pity about the drawing. "We shouldn't still be talking shop," he apologized, "and trying to pick your brains, after this morning."

She looked unhappy. "I'm only sorry that it was no use."

"Not at all. But I sincerely regret the necessity for asking you to go to a mortuary and view a body. Most unpleasant."

"Oh," disclaimed Miss Seeton, "I didn't mind that. Though, of course," she added, "it's not what one would choose. I saw several when I was young—bodies, I mean—though those, naturally, were being cut up."

"Naturally." Sir Hubert sounded, was, defeated. It might be *Wonderland* for the sergeant but, for him, it was *Through the Looking Glass*. Purely Jabberwocky.

Sergeant Ranger sighed. The words were English, but the results were right off. How did the Oracle always understand her? She'd certainly gummed up old Sir Heavily.

"In hospital?" asked Delphick.

She turned to him gratefully. "Yes. Nowadays one can buy those clever figures, the visible man—woman, too; and I believe there are dogs—but in my day one had to rely on books and though, of course, they were most painstakingly drawn—the bones and muscles, I mean—it wasn't the same as the real thing. And anatomy is so important. It was very good of the hospital to allow me to attend the dissection classes."

"And you found that helped?" asked Sir Hubert.

"Well, no," admitted Miss Seeton. "At least, not as I'd hoped. The muscles and sinews, of course, were all there. But, somehow, they were lifeless. Like the drawings. You see," she explained, "they weren't moving."

In the silence that followed, suppressed temper deepened the color in Gosslin's face from rose to violet. Delphick studied the carpet. It was up to Sir Hubert: he got to his feet.

"No," he agreed, "they wouldn't be." His voice came out high. He walked to the window and changed key. "One could hardly expect them to be. Moving, I mean. And they certainly shouldn't be." He turned back into the room. "Naturally. Unnatural if they were really." His voice trailed away.

At this distance, at this angle, Miss Seeton's drawing looked different. "Why did you draw those lines across the face?" he demanded.

Miss Seeton was distressed. "I don't know. I didn't mean to. I …"

Sir Hubert's gaze remained on the sketch. "Curious, close to, it seemed meaningless; but from here it looks more like a postmark."

"Good God!" The sergeant leaned forward. There was a crack as his heel came down on the plate beneath his chair. Embarrassment was postponed by a buzz from a box on the assistant commissioner's desk.

Sir Hubert pressed a switch. "Yes?"

"The car to take Miss Seeton to Charing Cross Station, sir," the box announced. "And an officer waiting to take her down."

"Thank you."

Farewells completed and the door closed behind their visitor, Sergeant Ranger wilted under the combined stares of the three senior men. The assistant commissioner resumed his seat.

"Perhaps, Sergeant, you will be kind enough to enlighten us—to explain your excess of religious fervor."

"It was the post office, sir. The Lewisham post office."

"What about it?"

"It was raided, sir. Just recently."

"And?"

"Well—nothing, sir. It was the coincidence took me by surprise."

"A subpost office?"

"Yes, sir."

"Considering that subpost offices are raided at the rate of several a day, it would perhaps be even more surprising if it hadn't been." Sir Hubert's eyes fell to the drawing on his desk; lifted to stare at Delphick. He shook his head. "Nonsense, man. Can't be true. It's reaching." He looked back at the sketch. "The implication's absurd," he said slowly; then quickened: "And you, Sergeant, should be back on a beat for presuming to imagine a connection." He pressed a switch and addressed the box. "Find out in each division where we've had this latest series of child killings if there was a raid on a subpost office round about that time. Put different men on to phone the divisions. I want the answers at once."

"Sir?"

"Yes?" he snapped over his shoulder at Delphick.

"Any other incidents?" suggested the superintendent.

"Of course. And any other incidents," he told the box, "or anything unusual that occurred within, say, a week to ten days of the murder, and let me know immediately."

A few minutes later the box buzzed again. Without waiting for the assistant commissioner, it started to speak as his finger touched the switch.

"In all cases, sir," the box sounded excited, "subpost offices were raided within a mile radius of where a child was killed. The first ten days before the murder and the intervals have been getting shorter each time: the Lewisham raid was only five days ago. Brentwood, West Malling, and Richmond report slight increase in thefts from houses and flats in their areas during the same period. Wimbledon and Lewisham still checking and will report back."

Sir Hubert sighed. "Thank you." He switched off.

The four men remained at gaze. The intervals had been getting shorter … Chief Superintendent Gosslin voiced it:

"The pace is hotting up. Our chum's getting a taste for it. Can't hold it like he did. Not so sure about this pinching on the side, though. Doesn't seem to match." He looked down at Sir Hubert's desk and shook his head. "To think we mightn't've got on to it so soon if that daft little baggage hadn't doodled all over a face."

The interview with Dr. Knight had solved nothing: no sign of an anxiety neurosis; no sign of rheumatism; no sign of anything wrong with the reflexes, in fact the contrary; no sign of a strained muscle or ligament; no sign of anemia; no sign of the aftereffects of a stroke, nor reason to suspect that there had been one. A collection of negative signs and one lack of reason which told her nothing since reason told her that something was amiss and the reason for anxiety remained.

Miss Seeton walked back through the village considering ways and means. She must, she decided, resign from teaching at once instead of going back for the summer term. She would write to the headmistress tonight. It would be most unfair to Mrs. Benn to have a drawing mistress in control of a class who was unable to control her own hand. She could give a month's notice on her flat. But if she took the plunge, cut her connections with London, and settled in the village where the only profession she knew had no outlet, supposing that prices went up, as they did, and her income went down, as incomes do, how would she manage? Faced squarely, the answer was obvious. Learn another profession. But what? Could she, for instance, learn to type? Typists were always needed and one didn't necessarily have to be a secretary: people took in typing at home, like washing in the old days. Would it take very long to learn? she wondered. Though, of course, there would be the capital outlay on a machine. Again, she could do perfectly well without Martha and that would save something and if one could clean one's own house one could surely clean other people's and "someone to do the rough"—"obliging ladies" she believed they were called nowadays; how the language changed—were very difficult to find. The board in the post office was never without one or two notices saying DOMESTIC HELP WANTED, but you never saw one that began WANTED DOMESTIC WORK.

She smiled and said, "Good morning."

There was no reply. The face remained passive though fractionally the girl hesitated in passing and the frightened eyes shifted.

One of those young things in the car when Effie tried to run into the road. So very shy. Ah, yes, the post office, that reminded her, she was nearly out of coffee.

The coffee bought, Miss Seeton stopped to look at the books in the center display. So colorful, even lurid; though she'd found, on the whole, the less color the more readable. And, yes, here they were, she thought she'd remembered seeing them, *Mastery Books. Master Banking in 30 Minutes.* Surely not; and one wouldn't have very much confidence in the bank. Whereas to *Master Your Emotions in 30 Minutes* seemed unduly long. She scanned the remaining titles. Yes, there was one. *Master Typing in 30 Minutes.* She feared that it might take her rather longer than that. She carried the little book over to the counter. After all, it wasn't expensive and it should give one some idea. On her way out, she glanced at the notice board. Yes, there were three DOMESTIC HELP WANTED and—good gracious, what an odd coincidence. Surely very unusual—one WANTED DOMESTIC WORK.

Miss Seeton felt cheered. There was a spring in her step as she continued down the Street. There were always answers to one's problems if one looked for them. There was only one disadvantage, she decided, in leading an uneventful life, the mind tended to become inelastic.

Dr. Knight's view of Miss Seeton and her uneventful life was summed up in a request to his daughter after his patient had left: "Hasn't that oversized young man of yours in the police got an unsolved murder lying around somewhere? Failing any hornets' nest to stir up lately the little Seeton's found herself a gum tree and chased herself up it. I couldn't reach her. You might climb up after her, Anne, and see if you can talk her down."

"Anyone home?"

Miss Seeton opened the kitchen door and looked into the passage. "Oh, how very nice. I'm so sorry, but with the door shut I didn't hear the door. I was just making coffee, will you have some?"

"I? I'd love some." Anne Knight was finding her mission a little embarrassing. It was all very well for Dad to say talk her down, or talk her out of it, but how did you go about it? Miss Seeton struck her as far too sensible a person to imagine there was anything wrong when there wasn't. And if it was to do with a drawing that she couldn't do—or could only half do, or something—the trouble might lie in the drawing itself. It'd really be best to see it and try to judge from that. But how did you ask to see a drawing you weren't supposed to know about and then reassure the artist when you didn't know anything about art anyway?

Anne took the coffee tray from Miss Seeton and carried it into the sitting room. Miss Seeton poured.

Anne stirred her cup. Wade straight in would probably be best. "I—er, that is, Dad ..." She stopped. Miss Seeton looked inquiring. "Well, you know you saw Dad this morning?" Miss Seeton appeared surprised. "No, please," Anne went on quickly, "it's not a breach of medical etiquette. It's more—well, more doctor's instructions to the nurse. You see he felt you weren't quite satisfied or not quite happy about things and so he sent me along to see if I could be of any help."

"I see. Really how very kind to take so much trouble. But, Miss Knight ... Oh dear. Should it be Nurse Knight? Or Sister Knight? I'm never very clear about these things."

Her visitor smiled. "I'd rather it was Anne. It's something to do with drawing, isn't it?"

"Well, yes. In a way." Oh dear. How difficult. "That is, my right arm—or, perhaps, I should say the right side, the side of the drawing, I mean—won't work. It goes wrong every time. So I do feel there must be something wrong with the right. Right arm, that is." Miss Seeton thought it over. "Perhaps I haven't made it quite clear."

Anne laughed. "Well, no. Not quite. But surely this was all some days ago? You've been up to Scotland Yard since then and done a drawing for them. And that one was fine, so it can't be you who's wrong."

"Oh, but that was worse," Miss Seeton assured her, then paused. Should one discuss …? And then how did Miss—did Anne know?

The other read her thoughts. "But everyone knows that Scotland Yard sent down to fetch you. It's been the talk of the village."

"Stupid of me," admitted Miss Seeton. "I hadn't realized that people might notice."

"I'm afraid," Anne told her, "there was so much guessing about it that I rang Bob last night and asked him what was up. Of course he wouldn't tell me anything, you know what the police are—blotting paper. They soak up information but they never give it out."

"It was nothing important," explained Miss Seeton. "Simply that they needed a sort of Identikit drawing, as they hadn't got a photograph."

"And I don't know what you mean," pursued Anne, "by saying it was worse. Because Bob did let out that they're all cock-a-hoop over whatever it was you did and that the Oracle—I mean Superintendent Delphick—thinks you're the greatest thing since Rembrandt and of the two, I gather, he prefers your work."

"But ..."

"No buts about it. It's a fact. Something you did's given them some clue and they're all happy as beagles chasing after it."

Miss Seeton spread her hands. "I ... I just don't understand."

"D'you mean they didn't tell you?" Twenty-five years of experience exploded. "Men. They're quite impossible. Tell me," Anne put down her cup, "what exactly was it that started you worrying?"

"You see, I was trying to draw Effie Goffer. Martha had told me that Mrs. Goffer had asked for a portrait." She smiled. "Well, I believe Mrs. Goffer's exact words were that she couldn't see that it would do any harm really. But that's the trouble. It has. I thought eventually the best thing to do would be something fairy tale, with just a touch of Effie here and there. I tried three times, and each time it came out the same, only quite dreadful."

"May I look at it?" Miss Seeton wavered. "There's only one way to lay a ghost," urged Anne, "and that's to face it. Whatever you did in London seems to've been just what the doctor ordered, so let's see what a mere nurse can do with this one." Her hostess still hesitated. "Come on, bring forth your dead and we'll give them a decent burial."

Reluctantly Miss Seeton went to her writing desk, opened the bottom drawer, and took out a bulky portfolio. They laid it on the floor, untied the tapes, and squatted down beside it to examine the contents.

"I think I pushed them in somewhere near the bottom because they were horrid," said Miss Seeton. "But somehow

I didn't like to destroy them—at least, not until I understood what was wrong."

Anne, who was turning over the accumulation, suddenly gave a crow of delight. "When did you do this? It's heaven." Miss Seeton's face was pink: "this" was a cartoon of Sergeant Ranger, pop-eyed and wondering, in football rig, with striped stockings and a striped muffler streaming behind him in the wind as he ran even faster while the Red Queen, with Miss Seeton's face, one hand clutching his, the other her umbrella, ran before. "May I buy it? Please? It's terribly funny, but terribly like him too. Poor Bob, he does so often look like that."

Pinkness became pleasure. "You certainly can't buy it. But if you want it I'd be very happy to give it to you."

Impulsively Anne leaned forward and kissed her. "You're a darling."

Miss Seeton's flush deepened. "Fiddlesticks. And in any case your father was very kind to me this morning and then refused to let me pay, which was wrong of him and most embarrassing."

"He couldn't anyway," laughed Anne. "He doesn't take private patients any more, he works with the doctors at the Brettenden clinic, otherwise we only take emergencies. Come on," she started on the drawings again, "we haven't got to your weirdies yet. Oh!" She pulled out one of the sketches of Effie Goffer. From underneath Miss Seeton retrieved the other two. Oh … Anne wished she hadn't said, "Bring forth your dead." Because that was what they were. Obviously. Three portraits of death.

A knock sounded: Miss Seeton rose. Opening the front door, she studied the caller, enrapt. What interesting bones. Most unusual. And beautiful coloring. Beautifully applied. Except, of course, the eyes. "Yes?"

"Seeton?"

Miss Seeton blinked. "Why, yes. That is, I ..."

"Good." Mel Forby stepped forward. Miss Seeton backed.

"Who is it?" called Anne.

Miss Seeton turned to the waiting room. "Oh, Anne, don't bother with those, I'll see to them." Forgetting her visitor for a moment, she ran into the room, dropped to the floor and began to collect the drawings.

From the doorway Mel Forby watched them. It came back: the Seeton battle-ax took art classes. These must be a couple of the suckers: a dried-up spinster—green fields, blue skies, and maybe-cow off center—and a little—Anne reached for a sheet of cartridge paper—pardon her, a grown but tiny girl.

"Don't mind me. I'll wait." She looked around. Plenty of furniture, for God's sake. Still better get on terms—make like the natives. Though in this skirt ... Gingerly she lowered herself to the floor. "Just make like I'm not here, but when teacher comes back I'd like a word if that's okay by you."

Anne stared in astonishment. Then she and Miss Seeton spoke together.

"I'm sorry," said Anne, "but Miss Seeton didn't ..."

"I'm sorry," said Miss Seeton, "but I don't think I quite ..."

They looked at each other. Both said, "I'm sorry." Both stopped.

"Pardon me, I should have said. I'm from the *Daily Neg* ... Hey, hold it right there. Did you say Miss Seeton? That's ... never," Mel Forby pointed, "never tell me that's Miss Seeton?"

"But of course," said Anne.

Even Mel's brash façade was shaken. From her first days on a newspaper Mel Forby had recognized that nature was against her: she looked too soft; she was too soft. A genuine flair for clothes, a gift for writing intelligent comments and forecasts on fashion, had landed her a job. For a softy that was as far as it would go; always supposing that she could hold the job. Putty—that was her trouble. Soft as putty right through. She had studied her face. Putty could be remodeled. No—come to think of it the modeling wasn't all that bad. A good paint plan should put the face right—particularly the eyes. Wide wondering eyes were out for this racket; eye shadow and black liners would take care of it. Gentle manners and good speech would get her nowhere, she decided. She read the tougher American novels, attended the toughest American films. She practiced assiduously and the result though spurious was in its way effective. To alter someone's nature completely may not be possible, but constant cooking will hard-boil the softest egg. It is doubtful if by now even Mel Forby could gauge how much the original putty had finally hardened through exposure. She waved an apologetic hand. "You'll overlook it if I just die right here of shame. Have me swept out when the trash men call. And bill the editor of the *Daily Negative*, he got me into this and he can damn well pay to have me carried out."

"You're a reporter," accused Anne. "How could you burst in like this?"

Recovering, Mel gave her a wide grin. "Honey, that was no burst—just a stride-in. When I burst you wouldn't know what's hit you. Look," she reasoned, "take it easy. I was sent down here to pit my puny strength against some muscle-bound Amazon they call the Battling Brolly and told to stay here till I find what gives." She waved her hand toward Miss Seeton. "And then you give me that. I," said Mel, "give up."

Anne caught herself almost smiling back at this odd, engaging stranger. "Why can't poor Miss Seeton be left alone? It's not fair."

"Who asks for fair? Is life? If I take off, you'll get another. The penalty of fame is press. What's the story?"

"But there isn't a story," protested Anne.

"Don't give me that. I shopped around some in the village before I came on here and dug up enough dirt to fill the front page: Miss S had been arrested; she's out on bail; she's been let go for lack of evidence; she tried to kill some girl by slinging her under the wheels of a car ..."

"Effie!" exclaimed Anne. "That little horror. She'd make up any story."

Mel was watching Miss Seeton. "Say, don't look now," she murmured, "but what's she up to?"

Anne turned. Oblivious, Miss Seeton, whose yoga exercises had accustomed her to the floor, was sitting cross-legged. She had taken a sheet of paper and, with the cover of the portfolio as a drawing board, she was working absorbed.

"Hi, Miss S." Mell leaned forward, offered her hand. "Miss S? Mel Forby. Proud to know you."

Miss Seeton jumped up, penitent. "I'm sorry. How very rude of me. But so interesting. It seemed important to get it down. Quite dreadfully rude, I—" She looked at the tray. "I'll make some more coffee. It won't take a moment." She collected the cups, hesitated in the doorway feeling that perhaps she hadn't expressed herself well. She smiled. "The bones, I mean." She left.

"You know, she's cute. What's that with bones?"

Anne leaned over to see what Miss Seeton had been doing. "Your bones, I gather."

Mel joined her, studied the sketch: in flat, hard planes, Mel Forby's face built up to a pair of luminous, softly shadowed eyes. She moved to the mirror on the wall; reviewed her eye makeup—hard black lines. She shrugged. "So if I could look like that," she indicated the sketch, "where'd it get me? On the Street you've got to look tough, act tough, or go under."

A chuckle escaped Anne. "Well, you could always try looking like that, then acting tough. Sort of take them by surprise."

Mel lingered, looking, then left the mirror. An eyebrow lifted. "Honey," she reflected, "you've maybe, just maybe, got something."

On Miss Seeton's return with the coffee tray, Mel took it from her and pointedly set it on a low table by the fire. Miss Seeton knelt to add wood while Anne collected the drawings into the portfolio and kept it by her as they settled, this time in chairs.

Anne was worrying: the drawing of Effie Goffer worried her; the presence of Mel Forby worried her. How to get Miss Seeton alone? "What time's your train?" she asked.

The penciled eyebrows slanted. "If trouble's coming up, my job is troubleshooting. So no train, baby; guess you're stuck with me for the duration."

Miss Seeton put down the poker, took up the coffee pot. "Trouble? The duration?"

"Say we just take for a start the Lewisham morgue and then the Yard. What gave with those two trips of yours?"

Miss Seeton debated. Surely there could be no particular secret about that since Anne said the whole village knew. "They asked me to do a sort of Identikit drawing, because they had no photographs. And, apparently, they don't always find photographers very successful when they're dead. The subjects, I mean. Perhaps it might be best if you spoke to Superintendent Delphick about it," she suggested.

Anne was indignant. "You've no right to ask such questions."

"That so?" Mel rounded on her. "Getting news is my job. Get it straight or get it crooked—but I'll get it."

"That's the point," retorted Anne. "When you've got it, half the time it gets twisted. It seems to me all newspapers really want is bad news."

Mel laughed. "Sure. Bad news's good news—good new's no news. Presswise, that's the way it goes."

"But that's what I mean. In the long run your job has to be paid for by other people's feelings."

"Anne." Miss Seeton was distressed. "I can't believe that Miss Forby would do anything of the kind. In the way of distortion, that is. She has her work to do and, though I'm bound to admit that the newspapers sometimes do seem to concentrate on—well, yes, I suppose you could call it bad news—surely that must be, really, in a way, the fault of other people. After all, if it wasn't what they wanted, they wouldn't buy them, would they? The newspapers, I mean. If Miss Forby …"

"Make it Mel, Miss S. Born Amelia. Which left the choice; good works or bad intentions. Stuck a T in it. Now I'm stuck with it. So what? Everyone calls me Mel, my unfriends call me Dear Mel and enemies add Darling." She turned to Anne. "Look, baby, let's not fight. You're for Miss S, I'm for Miss S, so why the fire and fury?" Reluctantly Anne grinned. "With all the facts, we do our best to help—the most of us." Mel shrugged. "Without, we help ourselves.

My editor, God save him, said, 'It needs a woman's touch.' I'm getting what he means. Let's start over. What's with those pictures there you're sitting on," she pointed at the portfolio; her voice quivered with laughter, "like you're a tigress in defense of cubs? I miss my guess or from the look of things there's something—something there that's got you buffaloed."

Anne was startled, Miss Seeton sharp. "No. Those," she explained, "are just odd notes and sketches, or impressions. There's nothing there to do with anybody else. They're purely personal."

Mel gave a joyous crow. "First time my face's been labeled pure and guess I'd always thought it personal to me."

"Oh dear." Miss Seeton looked sheepish. The bones, of course. She shouldn't have. So very ill-mannered; but it had seemed important. And such an unusual arrangement. The eyes, plainly, were a mistake. Superficial—but a mistake. Those hard black lines destroyed the theme. Quite wrong. But, naturally, one mustn't say so—be careful not to criticize. "Bones," she murmured, caught Mel's eye, got flustered, added hurriedly, "but not the eyes, naturally. Quite wrong." She bit her lip.

"Yeah, honey," agreed Mel, "we did kinda get the point about the eyes."

Unexpectedly Anne giggled, dragged forward the portfolio and opened it. She glanced at Miss Seeton for permission. "I think we'd better, don't you? We're not going to get rid of her," and she made a face at Mel, "so we'll have to trust her. Wait a minute, there's something ..." She pounced on a watercolor of Plummergen Church, painstaking and dull. She flipped it over on to Miss Seeton's lap. On the reverse side in quick, carefree strokes Mel Forby's face leaped from the paper. "Do you see?" Anne pointed in triumph. "Now will you admit there's nothing wrong with you?"

Miss Seeton considered it; a weight lifted, she felt renewed. Of course it was only rough, a note carelessly done, but at least it was complete. Not like those others. And that meant …

Mel Forby had sorted the drawings into two lots. The larger pile, the earnest, ineffectual children of care, she pushed to one side with her foot. "Trash," she observed. Anne's head jerked up, ready for quick defense. She saw the expression on Miss Seeton's face and protest became stillborn. Miss Seeton could appreciate another artist, active or passive, whether engaged on work or criticism, and her fleeting smile was one of understanding. Mel Forby, unaware of rudeness and innocent of the intention, was absorbed. She had an awareness of art, and to see so much plebeian work where occasional quick sketches showed the spark of genuine talent to her was sacrilege. "Run of the mill," she continued with impatience, "just wasted effort. But these—" she picked up a collection of line sketches, cartoons, and caricatures which included those of Sergeant Ranger and Effie Goffer; "these are something else again. These are really something. Want a job, Miss S?" she suggested. "Like me to show them to the art editor?" Embarrassed, but pleased, Miss Seeton shook her head.

Anne grabbed one of the Effie portraits. "Tell me," she asked, "the Lewisham drawing, was it anything like this?"

"Why, no." Miss Seeton frowned. Anne had said that the other had proved helpful after all; though frankly she couldn't see how. But it did imply that one ought to be accurate—try to remember. It had been so worrying and disappointing at the time that she hadn't really noticed. "The other was very messy," she apologized. "And then, I'm afraid, I sort of crossed it out." Unconsciously her fingers began to trace the air. "But perhaps," it became clearer, "I may be imagining it, but I think—yes, there was a difference in the two sides of the face."

"Then if you don't mind," said Anne, "I'll send one of these to Bob. If you had the same trouble over both of them, don't you think there might be a connection of some kind?"

"To Bob?" Mel Forby held up the Alice caricature. "You mean the Oracle's sidekick?"

Anne laughed and reached. "I'll take that too." Her gaze lingered on it. "Miss Seeton gave it to me, it's mine."

"So's he, looks like," remarked Mel, watching her. "Congratulations; he's quite a lot of man." Her eyes were dreamy, her mouth mocking. "Tell me—I'm a sucker for romance—just between us girls, does he give you that burning sensation in your midsection?" Anne balked for a second; then her eyes twinkled and she nodded. Mel stood up. "I guessed it was like that," she observed. "I've been there in my time; don't let it fool you, baby, it's ulcers, take bicarb. I'll do my best for you, Miss S. We'll keep these under wraps," she indicated the drawings, "and see how it pans out. But news is news no matter what. I'll do a kind of introduction—shift the focus. Try to switch the pitch."

* * *

From the *Daily Negative*—March 21

THE PEACE OF THE ENGLISH COUNTRYSIDE

by Amelita Forby

*

Piece 1. *Umbrella Cover*

To our armed forces it is air cover in time of war, to the cosmopolitan—gay beaches, to the Continental—cafés, to the golfer—colorful protection; but to the greater majority of us the word "umbrella" conjures up gray visions of city streets crowded with glistening black mushrooms under sluicing rain.

Here in the peaceful depths of the rural English countryside, in this tiny Kentish village of Plummergen in England's garden, the word has another connotation: for here it is that in a small cottage is stabled that most famous of all umbrellas—the Battling Brolly.

Last year many people in perusal of their daily papers acquired the erroneously false impression that the Battling Brolly was a woman.

Inexact. Of powerful personality, of adventurous disposition, a battler for the right, black-silked, steel-spoked, crook-handled, rumor hath it that this memorable gamp is on the move again.

Sensational developments are to be confidently anticipated and …

* * *

Chapter 4

Their tribal feuds and internecine strife laid by, the village needed new disport.

Although old Mr. Dunnihoe had held out as long as he could and longer than could be expected, his death a few weeks before had caused a humiliating drop in the population figures. It could be argued that the differential between four hundred and ninety-nine and five hundred was numerically only one digit; the difference in the look of the thing was great. And it was the look of the thing that counted. Now, with two new arrivals who had moved into the Dunnihoe cottage down by the canal, Mrs. Scillicough expecting and from the look of that it was evens on twins and four to one on a litter, the population of Plummergen was safely back in the five hundreds. A young couple with the girl's little brother had rented that ramshackle bungalow Saturday Stop out near the Common beyond the council houses. There was a visitor at the George and Dragon. Miss Seeton had returned. All in all there was plenty of new material upon which to embroider.

The trio at Saturday Stop were a success. The young man looked pleasant although little was seen of him, which was natural since he would be at work. What work was still uncertain but two days was short notice even for Plummergen to have completed a dossier on a newcomer. The little boy was found to be attractive with a sunny smile and good manners. That he was deaf and dumb was sad but it made him an ideal subject for patronage, and if he resented the shoulder and head pattings he was unable to say so since his attempts at speech were for the most part unintelligible. His elder sister was completely charming: the completion of her charm being the notice on the post-office board, WANTED DOMESTIC WORK. Her open face and good manner were felt to be reference enough and the response to her advertisement had been substantial; competition for her services was keen. She solved the problem, granting two hours here and two hours there, mornings and afternoons, by arranging to oblige eight households a week. It was to be hoped that the family might decide to extend their stay beyond their three months' lease or even to settle permanently in the village.

The pair at the Dunnihoe cottage were viewed with disfavor. They were very young, of sullen mien and of retiring disposition; infractions of custom of which the last was the most significant since at no time of life could there be honorable excuse, only dishonorable reason, for keeping yourself to yourself. Their extreme youth, seventeen or eighteen at most, coupled with the prefix Mr. and Mrs., made them untrustworthy. They could be married, no one was prepared to deny the possibility, but at that age it was "really too unlikely, wasn't it?" The boy's appearance was variously described as mumpish, not a good type, a wrong'un if ever I saw one, and "really too churlish." The girl was dubbed silly, scared, scared-silly and "it's too obvious he beats her." In the week since their arrival they had avoided or ignored such friendly, impersonal overtures as "How old are you?" "When were you married?" "Where do you come from?" "Why did you come to Plummergen?" and "What do you do?" This completed their damnation. The vicar's sister reported after a duty call that she found them clean, tidy, and very reserved. She was clearly influenced by her friend Miss Seeton, whose verdict of "shy" was ridiculous. Their contact with Miss Seeton counted against them. She had been seen in earnest conversation with them after that quite dreadful episode of Effie Goffer and the car; also she had been observed speaking to the girl on the Street.

The visitor to the George and Dragon was in a different category. She talked to everyone, asked questions and, unusual and therefore suspect, listened to the answers. Her speech came from films; her clothes, too unsuitable, and her makeup placed her as an actress. Someone who had read the registrar at the inn recognized the name Amelita Forby as that of the fashion writer in the *Daily Negative*, so in all probability she was a model which was the same as being an actress only worse. Her arrival on the same evening that Miss Seeton returned from London gave rise to speculation: she was a policewoman in disguise, or if the model story was true, someone hired by the police to keep an eye on Miss Seeton; she was a confederate from London; a member of a rival gang; certainly her own story that she was a reporter on a job could be discounted—there was nothing to report. As for that rubbish in the *Negative;* the less said about it the better. They'd had enough of umbrellas last year. Some connection with Miss Seeton was palpable. This Miss Forby, if that was indeed her name, had called at Sweetbriars at the first opportunity, staying nearly an hour, and the fact that Anne

Knight parried all attempts to discover the subject of such a prolonged conversation shed a sinister light upon the visit.

Sinister. Bob Ranger let out a small yelp of surprise and laid the drawing on his desk.

Delphick, entering, turned on his way across the office. “If you’ve got hiccups, drink water with your ears shut.” He tossed down a newspaper, sat, glanced through the in-tray, picked up his post. “What’s a fashion writer doing in Plummergen? And how did the *Negative* get on to it?” he asked. Bob started. “You don’t read the *Negative?*”

“No sir.”

Delphick threw over his copy. “Page two.”

With a growing feeling of helplessness, Bob settled down to read “Umbrella Cover.” It was going to be one of those days, he decided. Funny. Just the mention of Miss Seeton’s name and everything began to go backwards. The Oracle making bright early-morning chat about drinking with your ears; the press starting up the Battling Brolly again; and—this. He pushed the newspaper aside and studied the drawing anew. He’d been surprised to see Anne’s writing. She’d never written to him at the Yard before. And at that it was more of a note than a letter. Just: *Darling, don’t like this drawing of Miss S’s*—who could?—*Thought you’d better see it and show it to the Oracle if you think.*—Think what?—*She was trying to draw a child in the village and it went wrong*—he’d say it had—*like this three times.* Three ...? He glanced across the room. A small cloud was hovering over the Oracle’s desk. He’d hang on a minute.

Delphick picked up a telephone receiver. There was a slight edge to his voice. “Accounts, please.” While waiting he smoothed out a torn envelope and reread the contents. "Accounts? Superintendent Delphick speaking." … "Good morning." … "Yes, you can. I have a check here made out to, and the envelope addressed to, Mrs. Delphick." Bob was enthralled. "The number?" Delphick asked. He looked at the check. "O nine four six two seven double one." He smiled thinly at his fascinated sergeant. "They say it won't take a moment. They'll check the file." He returned to the telephone. "Good. And what has your file to say on the subject?" … "I see. Then if, as you say, it's correct, can I speak to whoever's responsible for the file?" … "I can't?" … "Oh, I see." He glanced across at Bob. "Computers can't speak," he informed him. "Perhaps," he suggested to the telephone, "you would be kind enough to come up yourself and speak on its behalf. The matter must be put right—and if you explain to me, and I explain to you, and you explain to it, then maybe we'll get somewhere." … "Thank you." He replaced the receiver and shook his head. "We are in danger, Bob. Our life, our livelihood, our manhood, all are threatened. They have installed a new monster in the basement which can dispose of us at will. It can marry us, divorce us, and generally play the hell with us, but we can't argue with it because it can't speak." He turned to his in-tray and paper work until there was a knock on the door. "Come in."

A member of the uniformed branch approached his desk and handed him a slip of paper. "That's the original memo we had, sir, so that's what we fed it."

"Fed it?"

"You feed it cards, sir, like—like you'd feed biscuits to an animal. It sort of digests them and comes up with the stuff." His eyes shone with enthusiasm. "It's infallible, sir."

"I see." Delphick considered the slip. "Was this information phoned to you?"

"That's right, sir."

"All is now clear, though evidently the diction wasn't. For Delphick's Missus try Delphick's Miss S."

Notebook and pen appeared. "Beg pardon, sir, you Missus, you said?"

Delphick clung to patience. "No. Miss S. The check should have been made out to a Miss Seeton." He encountered a blank stare. He began to feel desperate. "Can't you see? Miss S. It stands for Miss Seeton, man. Capital M i double s capital E double s, MissEss. Have you got it?"

"Yes, sir, I've got that clear, sir."

"Good. And the address is Sweetbriars, Plummergen, Kent. Now if you'll write all that on a biscuit and feed it to your infernal machine, we'll be straight." He met a dubious look. "Shan't we?"

"I hope so, sir. It doesn't like changing its mind once it's made it up, but I expect it'll be all right. It's infallible, sir."

"Thank you." The man departed. "And you, Bob," added Delphick as the door closed, "can wipe that smirk off." He leaned back and chuckled. "Delphick's Missus. can you see poor Miss Seeton's face?"

Bob could. It hovered in the air like a gentle, daunting ghost. How did she do it? She'd even got the accounts department going all poopsie by remote control. He'd been right. It was going to be a Seeton morning. Everything was going to be off. Right off.

The superintendent broke in on his reflections. "Bring me the files again." Bob leaned down and opened the bottom drawer. "We can only go on plugging at it in case there's any point we've missed. And there's always the chance there's a couple of words or so I don't know by heart."

The files on the child murder cases had grown fat. It was now more of a certainty than a guess that they and the post-office raids were connected. They had testimonies from over seventy witnesses at the five post offices involved and out of all the contradictions a picture had emerged. Two men: one of average height, one small; dressed in black, possibly leather, but the probability was black overalls; helmeted; goggled, with black masks or, more likely, black material hanging from the goggles. They arrived and made their getaway on motorcycles. The taller of the two held a gun and gave orders. The shorter one never spoke, but collected the haul and made off while his companion covered his retreat before leaving in his turn, threatening to shoot anyone who attempted pursuit. Unfortunately, no clue to their identities had been discovered. The thefts from flats and private houses appeared to have no connection with the killings or the raids although Delphick kept an open mind. They seemed to be casual and clueless as such thefts frequently were and the only householder who had any definite suspicions had too many: she was convinced that a temporary daily help whom she had employed had been involved, but since she was almost equally certain that her lodger, a neighbor with whom she had quarreled, and the milk delivery man whose manner she disliked had been equally guilty, whether separately or collectively she was unable to make up her mind, her suspicions could be discounted. There was little the police could do except wait for the next post-office raid that matched in method, converge on the locality, and try to set a trap for the killer.

Back at his desk, Bob looked at Miss Seeton's sketch again. Perhaps if he didn't show it to the Oracle everything would settle down. After all, Anne only said show it to the Oracle if he thought. That was it. He didn't think. He'd sit on it and say nothing. He picked up the sketch and Anne's letter, went over and laid the picture across one of the files on Delphick's desk. Delphick froze, staring at the drawing. He held out his hand. Unwillingly Bob passed him Anne's letter, comforting himself that except for the *darling* it wasn't very personal, but it did mention *the Oracle* and that would be—well, was—a bit off in itself. Delphick read it and reached for a phone.

"Ashford, Kent. Chief Detective Inspector Brinton. And rush it, please." He picked up another phone. "Chief Superintendent Gosslin, please." … "Chief? Delphick here. Another of Miss Seeton's drawings has cropped up. I think it's urgent. Looks like Plummergen's our next. Is the A.C. available?" … "Right." He put the receiver down. The first phone squawked. "Chris? Delphick. I've reason to think there may be a raid on the post office at Plummergen. Could you ring them and give them warning?" … "No, I don't know when. Probably within the next few days." … "Right. I'll hold on." He looked at Bob. "You don't know anything more about this? Miss Knight hasn't mentioned it before or spoken about it on the phone or anything?"

"No, sir."

The second phone rang. He picked it up. "Superintendent Delphick." … "Oh—yes, sir." … "Yes, it's here on my desk." … "Right, sir. But may I wait a few minutes? I'm holding on to Ashford while they get through to Plummergen post office." … "But I shouldn't be long—" … "Very good, sir." He put back the phone. "The A.C.'s coming down."

Bob returned to his desk. What else? Naturally old Sir Heavily would come to the Oracle instead of the other way about. Once Miss Seeton started mixing it, it was bound to be upside down.

"But there must be an answer. It's a post office," protested Delphick into the first phone. "If it was out of order, it'd've been reported." … "Right, I'll hold while you get on to the engineers." He swung round excited. "Bob, this may be it. D'you realize what's happening?"

"Yes, sir." Bob was resigned. "Miss Seeton's at it again."

The door opened. Sir Hubert Everleigh closed it behind him and walked straight to Delphick's desk. The superintendent began to rise but was waved down. For some moments Sir Hubert stared at the sketch. "How did you get this?"

"You remember Sergeant Ranger, sir?"

"Our lay preacher? Indeed, yes." Sir Hubert nodded to Bob. "The young man who adds two and two and gets religion."

"The drawing arrived by post this morning." Delphick held up Bob's letter. "You mind?" Mute, Bob shook his head. Delphick handed the letter to the assistant commissioner.

A smile flickered on Sir Hubert's face as he read it. The catalyst was working. "Who is this child? Do we know?"

"No, sir, not—" The phone reawoke. "There isn't?" Delphick looked grim. "Then I'd get cars out there if I—" … "You have. Good man. Now, Chris, more important. There's a child in Plummergen—I don't know who she is but you can get her name from Miss Seeton—" The telephone quacked. "Pipe down. If you prefer, you can find out from the doctor's daughter at the nursing home just outside the village, Miss Knight. That child might be—just might be—the next victim on our list." … "I probably shall. I—" Seeing the A.C.'s extended arm, Delphick handed over the protesting receiver.

"This is Sir Hubert Everleigh, Assistant Commissioner, Crime." The protests died abruptly. "I think the superintendent may well be right. I'd advise a round-the-clock watch on this little girl. We're guessing, but there's good foundation for our guess. And if there is trouble at that post office I'd say it was a near certainty." The telephone made polite suggestions. "Er—yes." Sir Hubert was distracted for a moment by Bob collecting the files from Delphick's desk and stowing them in a briefcase. "I was going to propose that. If you'd book them in at wherever it is they stay in the village, I should be grateful. I'll make all arrangements this end and get them off to you within the hour." … "Thank you—" he read out the words that Delphick had written for him on a piece of paper. "Chief Inspector Brinton. Good-bye."

Food, cooked and uncooked, books, clothes, toys, china, and glass. Call it a post office? Rats, it was Harrods without the walking. If she was going to be stuck down here for all time, Miss S would need more ashtrays. Just one for guests and carting it about was out. Mel Forby studied the display. The green one or the pink? Well, she guessed both. She picked up the green one to check the price.

The shop door was flung open and two motorcyclists rushed in.

Startled, Miss Nuttel dropped a bag of coffee beans. It broke. Another shopper gasped, one squeaked.

The door was closed.

Motorcyclists? Nuts, they were …

"Holdup," growled the taller with the gun. "Anyone moves, they get it. Make it quick."

The green ashtray went sailing, missed and landed behind the gunman with a crash. There was a loud report followed by a phut. Mel went rigid: her eyes slanted down to her hat lying near her feet. Back of her, a young, terrified assistant stood still, unconscious of condensed tomato dripping on to her head from a punctured tin on a shelf above her.

The shorter of the two raiders, bulky in black overalls, boots, the head disfigured by the crash helmet, by the dark goggles from which depended black material tucked in at the neck, walked straight to the postal grid to the rear of the ham and cheese counter. The telephone bell began to ring. Mr. Stillman, who had been serving a customer with grated cheddar, was about to lower the cardboard carton that he held.

"Forget it," snarled the gunman. Mr. Stillman forgot it.

His wife, serving at the grid, stared in helpless fright.

"It's all right, Elsie. I'll see to it." He addressed the figure by the door. "I've got the safe keys. We don't want trouble."

"Good. Put some snap in it."

The few lunchtime shoppers and the assistants stood like waxworks as Mr. Stillman, carton in hand, moved behind the grid. He swept the stamps and postal orders from the counter, knelt, put the carton on the floor, there was a jangle of keys, the sound of the safe opening, the clink of coins, a rustle of paper. In a few seconds he was upright again, slammed the carton onto the counter; quickly, automatically, he pulled at a roll of sticky tape and snapped a length across the carton flaps sealing it—across a postal order which protruded. Reaching high he handed it over the grid to the waiting black gauntlets. The telephone bell was ringing. The smaller raider took the carton, went to the door, opened it, ran out. The gunman closed the door; stood waiting. All stayed immobile save Miss Nuttel. Tall and angular, she swayed, eyes fixed in horror on the girl assistant with streams of red down hair and face and dress. Swaying still, green-white lips parted:

"Wha-, wha-, wha ...?" she said and crumpled to the floor among the coffee beans.

The telephone bell was ringing.

* * *

Stamps. How stupid. She knew there was something. She could, of course, get them this afternoon. But if she did, would she remember? She'd told Stan that she would weed the rose beds today and when you started on that it was teatime before you knew where you were and then she'd miss the post. Not that it really mattered. But once a letter was written, it never really felt written, if one knew what one meant, until it was sent. Since she had decided, finally, to go back to the school for the summer term and then to retire, now that she was sure she could manage, one way or another, the sooner the letter got off to Mrs. Benn the better. Yes, perhaps, on the whole, it would be best if she went now and she could post the letter at the same time. Miss Seeton turned down the thermostat to leave the stew simmering. Really, they should mark them better. Where it said "simmer" things always boiled. Whereas simmer was really where "on" was. And then she'd have the whole afternoon to concentrate on weeds. Well, it was grass mostly. She went upstairs to put on her hat and stood looking out the bedroom window. The chapter "Winter—Spring" in *Greenfinger Points the Way* said that grass lay dormant till

April and didn't need touching. But hers didn't. Lie dormant, that was. The lawn was looking a little rough and tufts of grass in the beds were growing strongly and were mostly in flower, or pod, or whatever it was called when grass did it. Downstairs she collected her coat, picked up her umbrella, and put Mrs. Benn's letter in her handbag.

The Street was deserted. Of course. Everyone would be at lunch. How lucky that Mr. Stillman kept open—nobody else did. Just one small figure standing by two motorcycles outside the post office. Oh, yes, she could see now: it was the one that was deaf and dumb; so very unfortunate; such a handicap. But, surely, it would be better if he were sent to one of those clever schools where they taught them. Quite brilliant, she believed. They started by teaching them to hear—though how, when they couldn't, one couldn't quite see. And then, from that, they learned to speak. Many, she understood, became so clever at it that one would never know. And, if they weren't taught, it must leave them so dependent. Which couldn't be good for them.

Miss Seeton turned to enter the shop, when the door was thrown open and a motorcyclist dressed in black ran into her. Miss Seeton sprawled, dropping her umbrella. She grabbed and caught it by the ferrule, the handle caught an ankle and the motorcyclist also sprawled, dropping a parcel close to her. Miss Seeton pushed it toward the cyclist.

"Your shopping."

The black figure scrambled to its feet. In the distance sounded the forlorn, two-toned mating call of a police car. Back still toward her, the cyclist hesitated, then leaped for one of the machines. A stutter, a roar, and cycle and rider raced southward down the Street.

Really. So very impetuous. On hands and knees, Miss Seeton prepared to rise when the door swung open and another figure charged out, tripped over her; an explosion, something fell with a clunk beside her, a shattering from across the Street followed by clatter as a plate-glass window at Lilikot disintegrated and the motorcyclist flying spread-eagled crash-landed on the curb. A telephone bell was ringing. The police car sounded nearer. The gunman, gunless, jumped up, ran for his machine. Another stutter, another roar, and he fled after his companion.

No, really. She didn't see how she could have avoided … She was, of course, very sorry that they had both been knocked down but no, truthfully, she couldn't feel that it had been entirely her fault. Miss Seeton picked herself up and dusted herself off. Now where was …? Oh. She stooped to retrieve a pistol lying near her feet. Holding it she remembered that very loud bang. How dangerous. And where on earth was the parcel that they'd dropped? A small figure was walking away, the carton under his arm.

"Wait. You can't take that, it isn't yours."

Of course. He couldn't hear. She caught his arm with her umbrella, turning him. They faced each other: he clung to the parcel; she shook her head, proffered her left hand, her right hand held the pistol pointed at his chest. Almost he defied her: the childish face changed; hardened and aged; a mask matured in hatred. The brief change was shocking for this new visor became reality, making the childish face appear the camouflage. Viciously he thrust the carton at her, turned and ran.

A parcel with a postal order sticking out? A gun? It—it couldn't be … No, No, surely not. One read about such things, of course, but not in the country. And most certainly not in a small village. But … Somewhat disturbed Miss Seeton approached the door. One wouldn't, of course, mention it openly in the shop, one didn't want to alarm people, but she'd have a quiet word with Mr. Stillman, he'd be sure to know.

The first police car, from the Brettenden Road, raced into the Street, blue light flashing, its siren burping like an operatic diva in distress, and pulled up in time to see a small elderly lady, hat askew, handbag and umbrella hanging on her arm, a parcel in one hand, a pistol at the ready in the other, walk into the post office.

* * *

From the *Daily Negative*—March 23

THE PEACE OF THE ENGLISH COUNTRYSIDE
by Amelita Forby

*

Piece 2. *Hard Cheese*

Sensational developments occurred here today when the slumberous lunchtime peace was rudely shattered by armed gunmen in a raid on Plummergen Post Office. Shots were exchanged for ashtrays. Women fainted …

… but Postmaster Mr. Stillman, aged 55, gray-haired, height 5' 9", matched force with guile. Disturbed when serving grated cheese, he …

… the takings on the floor and handed them the sealed carton filled with cheese plus one postal order. Even this they lost, for outside the shop the Battling Brolly was ready to immediately and without thought for personal safety go into action. A left hook, a short jab, and booty and gun discarded, the gunmen were routed.

Police were on the scene within seconds, but so far no trace of the raiders has been discovered.

The gun captured and the cheese returned, the only casualties were one ashtray, one tin of condensed tomato and—MY HAT (two holes in it).

Chapter 5

"… forever and ever. Amen."

The vicar ended the Lord's Prayer and took his seat. In the village hall the rest of the Parochial Church Council settled themselves with the whispered overwrapping of coats and mufflers for two hours of drafts and discomfort. The minutes were read and signed. Matters arising, such as main drainage, cracks in the bells, and the impassioned choice between a new mower and sheep in the churchyard, were summarily dealt with. Excuses for nonattendance were read or reported. Now at last the council was ready for the agenda, correspondence, and new matters for discussion. In short, the field was cleared, the lists were open, and jousting could begin.

Mr. and Mrs. Hosigg, the very young couple from the Dunnihoe cottage, were put up like dummies in a tiltyard. This gave everyone a chance to limber up and try a few practice runs without opposition, since the Hosiggs had no champion. He had some odd job. Driving a lorry or something. Or so it was said. If she looked frightened, there must be a good reason. He was sometimes away for days at a time. Nights, too. In fact he was very seldom there at night, it was believed. Actually nobody could say where he was at any particular time. If he drove a lorry by night, there was surely nothing to stop him riding a motorcycle by day. And if the girl looked frightened, there must be some very good reason indeed. You had to admit it was too peculiar.

"Should say he'd got a prison record, myself."

This thrust by Miss Nuttel brought protests, being judged a low hit and the weapon not properly blunted. Miss Nuttel retracted so far as to agree that appearances could be deceptive.

"Like tomato puree for blood?" asked Lady Colveden with interest, a lunge which unseated her opponent.

Norah Blaine jumped to her friend's assistance. "What Eric means is that from the look of him it's only too likely that he might have, which means that he'd know the sort of people who do that sort of thing. I mean he'd have friends."

This irrefutable logic concluded the trial by innuendo, Mr. Hosigg being found guilty of the post-office raid with a companion unspecified. The young Hosiggs were making the mistake of trying to live their lives independent of others. To assert independence is to defy convention, an insult which convention will repay.

Sir George Colveden said nothing, but decided that a job which took a boy away from his girl-wife for several nights a week was not quite the drill. He'd look into it.

Cheered by her success, Mrs. Blaine galloped back into the lists on a new hobbyhorse, a mare named Doris. Doris, the female of the species who had rented the bungalow Saturday Stop, had more supporters than detractors, six of the ladies whom she obliged being on the council. Such a brave girl. Always cheerful and willing. Doris had even suggested that she should clean the silver on Friday, most people wouldn't. So interested in everything, too, asking what was valuable so that she could take special care. Too nosy perhaps? Miss Nuttel was indignant and brusque.

"Certainly not. Nice gel. Works hard."

"She's too good to be true," agreed Mrs. Blaine. "Looking after that poor, handicapped little brother like that."

But couldn't the Welfare people …? No. Doris wouldn't hear of state aid. She preferred to be independent and manage for herself. Surely the husband …? Too sad. A breakdown and ordered complete rest by the doctors.

Sounded more like lead-swinging to Sir George. And the youngster ought to be at a school. Nothing known about them that he could see. And the girl in and out of half a dozen houses or more. No business of his, he supposed. Too good to be true … Probably the only sensible thing that Blaine woman'd ever said.

"Was it true," someone asked, "that there was some sort of trouble between Miss Seeton and the little deaf-and-dumb boy?"

There was a rustle round the table. Spectators leaned forward in order to miss nothing. Combatants looked to their weapons and prepared to take up positions behind their leaders. The main event of the evening had been heralded: The Post Office Raid and Miss Seeton.

"Yes, there was," charged Mrs. Blaine. "I know some people," she looked defiantly at Lady Colveden and Miss Treeves, "would say it's all coincidence. But you can't get away from her shooting our front window out—I might have been killed just as I was laying the table for lunch. And I suppose that would've been called coincidence too."

"Divine Providence," muttered Sir George.

"And then there she was," continued Mrs. Blaine, "standing in the Street, hitting that poor little boy with her umbrella."

"Considering," countercharged Lady Colveden, "that it was one of the raiders' guns which went off by accident when he fell, and hit your window, and nothing to do with Miss Seeton, don't you think you may be being just as silly about anything else you thought you saw?"

This exchange set the tone for the general engagement.

"If there's any trouble, she's sure to be at the bottom of it," was countered by, "Rubbish. If it hadn't been for her …" "I tell you there was money in it. I saw it. I was there," was denied by, "It was cheese." "There was no money in it when she brought it back, so where'd it gone?" was contradicted by, "It was never there." "Someone must have it." "Don't you read the papers?" "Making fun of the whole village." "Well, you can't blame …" "I can. If it wasn't for her …" "She was arrested going into the shop with a gun." "She saved everybody's lives." "But she fought the raiders single-handed." "She helped them escape." "If she wasn't one of them." "I knew …" "You couldn't …" "She did …" "We believed …" "You denied …"

"You can't deny," a Mrs. Farmint's shrill voice cut across the tumult, "there's no trouble except when she's here. Which proves she starts it."

"Poppycock," said Sir George. "Always trouble of some sort. When there isn't, you make it." Mrs. Farmint retired from the fray in tears.

An old echo of steel on steel; of horses' hoofs; of banners rippling in the wind, pennants fluttering on lances; of thrust, of parry, and of counterthrust. The chairman, the Rev. Arthur Treeves, listened in pained bewilderment. He had been saddened to hear that the newcomers to the Dunnihoe cottage were unsatisfactory, although he had failed to understand why. Had he seen them? He couldn't remember. Perhaps Molly … He'd ask her. He had been cheered to learn that the new people at Saturday Stop were so popular. And for such good reasons. Maybe they would elect to settle down in the village. They sounded so right. Arthur Treeves was an unworldly man; or at all events he lived in a world of his own, peopled by kindly folk who, since they did no evil, suffered no temptation to hear, nor see, nor speak it. As a priest, his weakness in doctrine was balanced by his strength in humanity. He saw his parishioners, when he saw them at all, and particularly if he remembered their names, as shining examples of the glory of Man. Had he given the matter consideration he would have been shocked to discover that he viewed the majority of the Ten Commandments as trifling peccadilloes which were strictly the affair of the people involved and no concern of his. When forced by circumstance, or by his sister, to acknowledge imperfection he could be roused. A case of unkindness, the only sin he recognized, would make him militant. Such a case was the post-office raid. It had taken Miss Treeves time and patience to explain to him that it was more than some slight difference of opinion over the price of cheese; that it was an actual robbery by force of arms and that shots had been fired. Robbery was unkind; force yet more unkind; but to shoot a gun, thereby endangering human life, was potentially the unkindest cut of all. Arthur Treeves was angry and determined to play his part in wiping such a stain from his parish. He had expected the raid to be the talking point of tonight's meeting and had been prepared to be stern. He had expected a chorus of praise for the courage of Miss Seeton, whom he admired, and had been ready to add his voice, but somehow the chorus, though loud, jangled sharp and out of key. He could not understand it. Nervously he fingered the pile of correspondence in front of him on the table; this too he could not fathom. They were mostly about Miss Seeton. In the letters she was variously described as Joan of Arc, as Mata Hari—some film star, he imagined, of whom he hadn't heard—as Florence Nightingale and as Jezebel—this last surely, whatever the writer's intentions, a serious misreading of the Old Testament. Finally, there was a cryptic communication from that old ex-colonel who lived next to the George and Dragon and spent most of his time there:

> *To the Parochial Church Council*
>
> *Sirs,*
>
> *Colonel Windup begs to inform you the woman's a damn nuisance.*

"The woman's a damn nuisance." Chief Detective Inspector Brinton of the Ashford Criminal Investigation Department looked up from studying Miss Seeton's sketch of Effie Goffer which lay upon his desk. "Listen, Oracle, take her back to London, we're not geared to cope with her capers down here. She ran the whole force ragged last summer, hibernated through the winter and now that spring is upon us, the sap is rising and she's hell-bent for another spree. The local chummies and we understand each other. They commit their little crimes and we commit the chummies in return. Fair enough and all quite matey. But one wave of that brolly of hers and it's CRIME in capitals. What's the matter with her? She's like a magnet. Crimes head for her like homing pigeons. Though I've never met the lady, it's my belief she starts it all herself out of sheer devilment."

Delphick laughed. "There you agree with the villagers. The general idea seems to be that what she doesn't do herself she's in cahoots with."

"Don't blame 'em." Brinton picked up a file marked Plummergen P.O., and began to leaf through it. "All right, you tell us there's going to be a post-office raid. Why? Because of this drawing." He prodded the sketch. "Though why you should think that proves anything, except that she can't draw, beats me. All right, we find the raid's already on. So all right, we send cars. They arrive and what do they find? Your girl friend marching into the post office with the oodle in one hand and a gun in the other. Caught red-handed and they arrest her. But no. Just because it's her, it has to be different. She's a heroine. She's just flipped two chummies over her left shoulder, taken their gun and the oodle away from them, and is bringing it back. And then because it's her it has to be different again and the oodle turns out to be cheese." The chief inspector laid the open file on the desk in front of him. "Oh, no, Oracle, we don't play in her league. Get her transferred."

"It's good for you, Chris," retorted Delphick. "She stretches the imagination—pretty far, I admit—and provides an outlet for your natural talents. And don't forget the A.C. takes that drawing you're so rude about pretty seriously too."

"Don't we all? I've got two men in plain clothes—God save me, have you seen 'em? In my day plain clothes were just a uniform in a different color. But these. Purple thises, pink thats and striped the others and they call 'em plain—trailing round after that little brat in shifts, and from the men's reports she's one of the nastiest little tykes spawned. If she does get herself done in, I'll arrest one or both of 'em and get a conviction on their reports alone. How serious do you want it? An armed battalion forming fours all round her?"

Delphick grinned. "Poor Chris. We'll take the men off as soon as I can get things organized. I want to lay a trap. It's the only way we'll get him. The only way in the long run we can make it safe for the girl herself."

"You really think, Oracle," Brinton glanced at the sketch again, "just on the strength of this, it's got to be this child?"

Delphick nodded. "Yes. In my own mind it's got to be her. Just on the strength of that."

The chief inspector shook his head. "So, you may be right—not saying you're not—but we've got some local talent here and the P.O. raid could've been just up their street and no connection with any murders, child or otherwise. They're a bunch that run together. They've all got motorbikes and call themselves the Ashford Choppers. Give 'em this, they live up to their names; bust up cinemas, and their favorite—we had one last week—wait till one of the villages or nearby towns have a Saturday hop, and the Choppers turn up, pick a fight with somebody, and tear the place apart."

"But it wasn't a bunch at the post office," objected Delphick. "There were only two."

"All right," conceded Brinton, "but they've got to graduate sometime—take up a career—and when they do they pair off, hit old women on the head for handbags, knock up small shops and pinch the till and cigarettes. This P.O. job would be just about their mark. Couple of beginners pinching cheese, then falling flat on their fannies and dropping it."

Delphick shook his head doubtfully. Brinton took a pen and made a note. "Well, me, I'll keep the Choppers in mind. But it's your case and I'm not beefing. Just tell us what you want."

The superintendent grew thoughtful. "You know, Chris, in my experience, when a small community like the village gets weaving on facts and fancies they start by taking the worst possible view of everybody and go on down from there. But, although they mostly get everything wrong, they often hit on a basic truth without knowing it. The thing that interests me in this case is that the raiders arrived on motorcycles; left on motorcycles. The obvious deduction being that they came from a distance. But everyone, even the sensible ones as far as I can make out, accept the view that it's an entirely local affair. And if it's the boys I'm after, and I'm pretty sure it is, that means it's got to be somebody who's only just arrived—someone new. And the only people who qualify are young Hosigg with ..." His voice trailed away.

Brinton watched the other's face for a moment before asking: "With what? You look as if you'd bitten on a lemon."

"I was thinking," said Delphick slowly, "of something Miss Seeton said at the Yard. Someone small and weak trying to prove themselves. Chris, could the smaller of the raiders, and all witnesses have always agreed that one was much smaller than the other, could that one be a girl?"

The chief inspector thought. "Yes. In that rig men and women look alike except for height. Could be."

"Because then," concluded Delphick, "it's equally probable that our killer is the girl."

"Oh. I see. Very nasty."

"So we're left with young Hosigg and his wife and another couple who've rented a bungalow somewhere there. I haven't got their names yet except that the girl's called Doris and she's got a little brother who's deaf and dumb."

"Quint's the name," Brinton told him. He turned a page in the file and ran his finger down it. "Yes, here we are. The second car to reach the P.O. came in from the south on the New Romney-Folkestone road. They report no motorbikes passed them. I don't know Plummergen well but there's a narrow bit of road at the end of the village ..."

"Next to Miss Seeton's," Delphick informed him.

"It would be. Anyway, the driver stationed himself there and questioned all cars coming into Plummergen from the south. Among them these Quints. They've got a small van and were out joy-riding with sandwiches during the girl's lunch hour."

Delphick looked up. "But I thought the little brother was near the post office."

Brinton turned the page. "Yes. A statement from Miss Seeton: At twelve-thirty-two approx. I was proceeding in a northerly direction along the Street ... Well, to translate it back into English: I saw this little blighter hanging about having a dekko at the bikes. When the oodle got dropped, he picked it up and tried to scarper with it and I collared him and snatched it back and Bob's your uncle. Probably not exactly her own words either, but that's what it boils down to. They tried to question him later through his sister who's the only one who seems to understand him but got nowhere. His version, according to her, is that he weren't doing nothing, just standing about, and Miss Seeton upped and bashed him one with her mush."

"What were these Quints doing having a picnic on a cold day in March?"

"Dunno. Maybe with baby brother underfoot she and hubby don't get much time together. Anyway, she says she gave the boy some sandwiches and left him to it while they set out to munch their bread and pickles off the Rye-Hastings Road. And neither they nor anyone else saw any bikes. Which leaves only," he flipped over some more pages, "the canal road to Rye, which isn't much used. And no wonder—it's potholed, wriggles like an eel, and is just about wide enough for one car. The only driver we've found along there at about the right time is a local van and he could easily've missed the bikes when he was delivering at one of the houses. Incidentally," he turned back a page, found his place, "yes, I thought so, your Hosiggs live down by the canal. They were questioned along with everyone else down that way in case they noticed anything. But no dice. The boy was asleep—he drives a lorry, mostly by night—and the girl says she was busy getting his lunch ready. The lads did a quick look-see while they were there and the couple own an old car, but no sign of any bikes."

Delphick got up, restless, and began to pace the office. "It's whittling down. But as regards the Goffer child, it's time we're up against and that's what worries me. Though she should be all right for the moment with your fancy-dress bodyguard. I'm a little worried about Miss Seeton too."

"About her?" The chief inspector was surprised. "I don't see there's anything to worry about there. And from what I've heard of her, if any chummies did take it into their heads to tackle her, they're likely to end up in hospital with a brolly through their linen basket."

The superintendent at the window watched the Ashford traffic unseeing. "It may be a bit farfetched, but I had a word with your village P.C., Potter. He's pretty bright, and his wife keeps her ear to the ground, works on church councils or something. The local idiots seem to've decided that Miss Seeton masterminded the raid in league with young Hosigg, then either double-crossed him and pinched the money herself or else staged the whole of her post-office act to cover his getaway and hold up pursuit."

"But there wasn't any money," protested Brinton, "only one postal order."

"I know. But that doesn't suit the village. They feel they've been made to look ridiculous in the eyes of the world. And the Forby's articles in the *Negative* haven't helped—and of course they blame poor Miss Seeton for those too. And for the fact that Forby's down here at all. They also blame her for our being about the place. In which of course they're right, but for the wrong reasons. Anyway, they've decided that large sums were stolen—I gather the postmaster gave a pretty convincing performance—because they feel that large sums are better for their civic pride."

"And where's the money supposed to be?"

"Oh, Miss Seeton's got it. Or, one of their brighter suggestions, she's got half and I've got the other half on condition I keep quiet."

Brinton guffawed. "I like that. I like that a lot. Can't I have a share? After all, as regards the raid, we've been doing most of the work down here. But I get what you mean. If the raiders hear it—and believe it—they'll be after her to get their oodle back."

"That," agreed Delphick, "is why I'm a bit worried."

So very fortunate. And, really, not painful at all. Though, of course, one's mouth still felt peculiar. Still, better than toothache. And, in any case, wisdom teeth were quite unnecessary. The dentist in London had warned her last year that he thought it was impacted, whatever that meant, and that if it gave her trouble it should come out. Well, it had—and now it was. She had found Mr. Geldson's name and address among Cousin Flora's papers, but dentists were always so busy she had been afraid it would have to wait until another day. But, no. On the phone Mr. Geldson had said at once that for any relative of Mrs. Bannet's he would manage somehow and, that if she could get over to Rye during the afternoon he would fit her in late. By catching the morning bus into Brettenden and having lunch there she had got here all right and the thing had been done. But now she would have to wait nearly three hours for a bus back. The eight-thirty would get her to Brettenden just in time to catch the evening bus back to Plummergen. She had rather hoped, with time on her hands, to have a look round Rye, such a charming old town, but Mr. Geldson had said no. He advised her not to open her mouth in the street and to keep indoors as much as possible so as to avoid catching a cold in the cavity, and had suggested that she should have a light meal somewhere and to take one of the two tablets he had given her, so that the tooth or, rather, to be accurate, the lack of it should not be painful when the injection wore off. The other tablet she was to take when she went to bed. Mr. Geldson had warned her that the tablets might incline one to feel a little drowsy and, on no account, must one take them with spirits. Well—that wasn't very likely.

This should do. Teas and Light Refreshments. She would have china tea, if they had it, an omelet and some toast—no, perhaps, in the circumstances, bread and butter would be wiser.

With some difficulty in enunciation, the meal was ordered, the omelet arrived, and Miss Seeton embarked upon it. The first forkful missed its mark.

Really, it was all very well Mr. Geldson saying "Have a light meal" but she didn't feel he quite appreciated the difficulties. After all, if one couldn't be sure where one's mouth was—and even less sure whether it was open or shut ... Perhaps if she tried on the other side and used her left hand. By the end of the omelet Miss Seeton had become quite expert, following each forkful with a quick administration of bread and butter. It was so much easier to tell where one was going with the hand rather than with the fork. Tea was really very awkward indeed. She managed a few sips, sufficient to wash down the tablet, then gave it up in embarrassment. Actually, Mr. Geldson's suggestion of a cinema was a wise one. One probably did not, in fact, look as grotesque as one felt, but in a cinema, where it would be dark, one would be less self-conscious. And it would, presumably, be warm. Miss Seeton paid her bill and went in search of entertainment.

Sheba. This should be interesting. One read so much about the accurate research they did on these historical films. In the darkened auditorium Miss Seeton stumbled over several invisible bodies and settled down in a vacant seat. How very convenient. There was a clock over some doors marked EXIT. She could keep an eye on it and if she left here at eight-fifteen it would give her ample time to get to the bus stop just down the road.

There was a loud clash of cymbals. On the screen appeared a long train embroidered with peacock feathers, which hung from the shoulders of a very blonde young lady who was standing at some distance.

"The Queen of Sheba, O King Solomon," declaimed a voice, "desires your acceptance of a few trifling gifts that she's brought."

The screen changed to a string of camels with several colored gentlemen, wearing loincloths, unstrapping large wooden chests and wicker hampers. These they carried with some difficulty toward an imposing palace. Miss Seeton nodded with satisfaction. So accurate: the long train of camels bearing many precious gifts. She settled farther down in her seat. It was beautifully warm in here and her mouth wasn't worrying her at all. Mr. Geldson had been quite right. She felt very relaxed. The colored gentlemen with the luggage skirted the main entrance to the palace and disappeared through a small door at the side. How odd. She wondered vaguely where they'd gone. Some sort of tradesmen's entrance probably. The very blonde young lady appeared again, much closer now. Blonde? But one would have expected that, as Queen of Saba—which, if she remembered correctly, was in South Arabia, near the Persian Gulf—the lady would have been comparatively dark-skinned. Or, at all events, dark-haired. But then, of course, many people thought of Cleopatra as a dark Egyptian, whereas the Ptolemies had, in fact, been almost pure Greek. Perhaps something of the same sort applied here. Also the peacock feathers struck her as strange. Miss Seeton blinked a little to bring the picture into focus. After all, the tail feathers of a peacock were a male perquisite and, since the Sabian religion worshipped the sun, moon, and stars, an embroidery of astronomical signs would have seemed more appropriate. She must borrow an encyclopedia from the library in Brettenden and look it up. The very blonde young lady raised an arm and smiled. Miss Seeton smiled in sympathy. Such a comfort, just at the moment, to see someone who evidently had no trouble with her teeth.

"Hail, Saarlyman," nasalized the very blonde young lady. "I've heard great reports of your wisdom, that it is the greatest, so I've come to test you," said the very blonde young lady.

The majestic figure of the king rose from his seat. Miss Seeton sank in hers. The king's face swam forward, huge, dominating. Miss Seeton blinked again. It remained a little blurred. Hooded eyes languished at her. Sensuous lips invited her.

"Your wisdom yet but sleeps," declared King Solomon. "Come, I will awake you."

Miss Seeton ignored the summons. Miss Seeton slept.

Where's Miss S? Gee, what in God's …? Mel Forby peered through a window of Sweetbriars at the ransacked living room. She tried the front door. Locked. She glanced through the window beyond into the small room opposite. The same. She spun and ran back to the George and Dragon.

Where's Miss Seeton? What the hell …? Bob Ranger stood in the doorway of Miss Seeton's sitting room and gazed at the mess. He had just returned from doing the rounds, asking questions, when that reporter woman had panted into the pub with the news. Followed by Mel, he had hurried round the cottage to find the back door locked but the window next to it open, a pane broken. Too small for him, he had boosted Mel through it and she, careful to touch nothing, had stepped across the jumbled kitchen into the passage, eased herself round the heavy oak door to the cupboard under the stairs of which the contents, a miscellany of coats, suitcases, brushes, cleaning materials and a vacuum cleaner, littered the floor and, finding the front door to be barred but not locked, had drawn the bolts and let him in. A slow burn began inside Bob. Privately he might think that the Oracle's MissEss was a bit off, he might have his own doubts about her. But that didn't give others a right to criticize her, let alone, be damned sure, anything like this. He ran upstairs. It was the same: cupboards opened, drawers pulled out, the contents spilled onto the floor, rugs thrown aside, carpets ripped back, pillows and cushions slashed. He went back to the living room and, using a handkerchief, picked up the telephone. Fingerprints—what a hope. He got through to Delphick at Ashford.

"Very good, sir. I'll wait till you get here and phone round Dr. Knight's, the Colvedens', the Treeves' and anybody else to see if I can get a line on her."

"Where's Miss Seeton? What on earth …?" "Where's Miss Seeton? What in heaven's name …?" "Bit of a shambles, what?" "Where …?" "What …?" And why?

Bob Ranger was beginning to feel like an attendant at a preview. Lady Colveden and Anne Knight had proved too much for him and, upon promise to disturb nothing, had gone over the cottage with paper and pencils talking notes as if preparing to bid at an auction, and had then retired to confer with Miss Treeves. Outside, in the fading daylight, the villagers were gathering, intrigued by the activity, brightly speculative. “Stabbed she’s been, I doubt above a dozen times.” “Done a bunk, like to be, with the post-office wad.” “Her throat cut right through near enough.” “Mutilated.” “Makes you wonder.” “Too horrible, of course, but what can you expect? I’ve always said …”

Where’s MissEss? What the devil …? A flick of wry humor shot through Delphick’s mind. That confounded nickname had popped up unexpectedly from his subconscious. With the scientific squad that had followed him from Ashford he made a thorough examination of the cottage. No classic clues presented themselves. No footprints, no cigarette stubs, or even ash, no tom scraps of paper with half a name and address, and of course no fingerprints. The knife used for slashing the cushions and mattress was from the kitchen. On the credit side, there was no sign of any struggle, though that proved nothing. The affair had all the earmarks of an unhurried but fruitless search and the superintendent sent the squad back to Ashford with several envelopes full of probably useless dust and fluff and two dark hairs, one found on the sofa in the sitting room and one on the floor in the bedroom, which looked to be from a human scalp and which might, or might not, prove something provided that they had no innocent explanation and provided that they ever found a head to which to match them. An inventory taken with Martha Bloomer produced the information that: shoes, she couldn’t be sure; and gloves she didn’t know; but that big handbag of hers, well more like a hold-all, really, that was missing; and one of her hats, the one with the bit that stuck up on top which you couldn’t mistake, that was gone; and so was her winter coat; the key to the kitchen door and the key to the door in the garden wall, they were gone too; and so, of course, was her brolly. Delphick felt comforted. It looked as if Miss Seeton had left under her own steam for wherever she'd gone and that the intruder or intruders had either watched her go or had arrived by chance in her absence. Most likely climbed over the low wall down by the hen houses, broken in, searched at leisure, and left by the way they'd come back on to the footpath by the canal. Somehow the umbrella clinched it. If abduction had been in question, he couldn't see even Miss Seeton insisting on taking her umbrella with her, nor could he imagine anyone with any knowledge of her reputation being so foolhardy as to allow her to do so. Nothing appeared to have been stolen but then there was nothing of any great value to attract thieves. No, on the whole, he thought his first guess had been right. It was the post-office raiders after what Chris called their oodle. And for that the villagers' passion for sensation was largely to blame.

The Colvedens arrived accompanied by Anne Knight in Sir George's enormous station wagon with an assortment of cushions, pillows, and a mattress. Miss Treeves came over from the vicarage to help and the cottage began to hum with activity. Martha fetched her husband, Stan, who cut a piece of glass from a spare cloche in the toolshed and repaired the kitchen window. A sibilance at the front door announced Miss Wicks.

"I shan't stop, but they said all poor Miss Seeton's things had been stolen and I wanted to be of some assistance so I brought my silk shawl in case it should be of service."

Lady Colveden was touched. She knew that the Chinese shawl was the old lady's most cherished possession, always worn at afternoon tea parties. But why should someone who whistled on their esses always choose such unfortunate words? And why, for one's own part, in conversation with Miss Wicks, should every word in the English language suddenly begin with ess? She braced herself. Not an ess would she utter.

"It's really very good of you indeed. I'm sure Miss Seeton ...?" Betrayed, she floundered.

Molly Treeves came to her aid. "How very, very kind of you, Miss Wicks. Miss Seeton is certain ..." In her turn she wavered.

"To be much moved," finished Lady Colveden.

In a glow of pleasure the old lady departed.

It should have been pandemonium, reflected Delphick. But it wasn't. Drawers had been repacked and put back, cupboards tidied and closed. Bob had been organized to tack carpets, to fetch and carry. All damaged articles were neatly stacked in the station wagon with a list ready for the insurance. Upstairs Lady Colveden and Anne Knight were remaking the bed on a fresh mattress. Downstairs new cushions were in place and Miss Treeves, having straightened the rugs, was vacuuming up feathers. In the kitchen Martha, whose panacea for all troubles was food, was making a stew—"she might want it tonight and if not it'll do for tomorrow's lunch regardless and all the better for staying over." At the kitchen sink Mel Forby, helped by Nigel Colveden, on whom the luminous, softly shadowed eyes copied from Miss Seeton's impression of her were evidently making an impression of their own, sliced onions, scraped carrots, peeled potatoes. Extraordinary, mused Delphick. People of good will producing order out of chaos with no fuss, in no time.

In the sitting room Sir George Colveden, with a large-scale map of the district spread on a table, had set up his divisional headquarters. Delphick had telephoned to Ashford and apprised the chief inspector of the situation. They had agreed that on the face of it there was nothing to worry about. Miss Seeton would almost certainly return on the last bus. Should she fail to do so they would alert patrols and institute a search. Further telephone calls made it appear unlikely that she had taken a train to London. At all events she had not been to her flat, nor to the school. And in any case she'd've been sure to tell Martha Bloomer of any such intention. The superintendent crossed the room to examine Sir George's plan of campaign. On the map a circle with a five-mile radius had been drawn with Plummergen as its center. The circle was quartered. Neat tracings had been taken of each quarter with, below, the make and registration number of the car allotted to that segment, the name of the driver, the name of the passenger. Nigel Colveden, he saw, was paired with the Forby. He frowned. Pity there was no way of keeping her out of this. The last thing they wanted was the press.

"Your son's got his own car then?"

"Gave him m'wife's little M.G. he was always borrowing. She's got a small Hillman now. More suitable."

Lady Colveden and Miss Treeves. Arthur Treeves with Sir George.

"Isn't the vicar a little old for this sort of thing?" he asked.

Sir George grunted. "Mad keen. If I don't take him we'll have the padre going off into the blue on his push-bike. Forget what he was doing after ten minutes. We'll've enough on our plate without having to round him up as well."

Bob was going with Anne Knight in the car she shared with her mother. Well, he'd agreed to that. It was a good idea as long as they kept their minds on the job, which, knowing them, they would. He himself would stay with the police car at the George and Dragon, in touch with Ashford and the patrols, and stand by ready to head in any direction if there was news. It'd be waste of a man to immobilize Bob as well. Delphick picked up a separate sheet marked POLICE: FOR USE OF. It listed the names of the cars, their sectors and occupants. You had to hand it to the military. When it came to planning they knew their job.

"Thank you, Sir George. This should save the patrols some unnecessary stopping and questioning. Though let's hope none of this will be needed."

"No. But if wanted, better to have it laid on. We don't want to boob, with a last-minute shambles and the cars all swanning around over the same ground. If she's not back on the bus, cars take off at twenty-two hours. And pack it in at o-thirty sharp. Two and a half hours's long enough for amateurs to concentrate in the dark. After that, sure to be an accident."

Chapter 6

"We turn left here. Then straight on along a curly bit. And then left again." Miss Treeves snapped off the flashlight as Lady Colveden followed the directions.

They had driven slowly to the northern limit of their sector and were now on the first return lap. They had seen no one on foot, one man on a bicycle, seven cars, and stopped twice to examine dark shadows which had proved to be dark shadows. Miss Treeves watched the shoulder, Lady Colveden watched the road. She hoped—she did so hope—nothing had happened. It couldn't have. The poor little thing must have gone somewhere and forgotten the time. But, if so, how would she get back? And it was so cold.

There was a loud clash of cymbals. Miss Seeton stirred. Through the mists of sleep voices murmured, pictures flickered. Miss Seeton shook her head to clear it and concentrated on the screen. A face swam forward, huge, dominating. Miss Seeton blinked in surprise. Hooded eyes languished at her. Sensuous lips invited her.

"Your wisdom yet but sleeps," declared the face. "Come, I will awake you."

Miss Seeton obeyed the summons. Miss Seeton sat up straight.

What a relief. For a moment she was almost afraid that she had dropped off. But, no, she remembered now. It was King Solomon and she'd seen him do it before. Before ...? She glanced at the clock over the exit doors. She shook her head again; looked again. Surely, it couldn't be, twenty to eleven. Oh dear, how truly dreadful. She must have slept right through the picture and round again. She jumped to her feet, stumbled over the three remaining patrons in her row, and hurried up the aisle. At the bus stop she read the timetable. It offered no hope until morning. What should she do? So extremely careless of her. Go to a hotel? But she'd nothing with her, not even a toothbrush. Remembering the cavity, she closed her mouth. Hire a taxi? But from where? And, in any case, surely it would be very expensive. Opposite her a signpost suggested London, Sevenoaks, Tunbridge Wells. Miss Seeton was turning away when a smaller arm to the post, pointing down a decline, caught her attention. It read: PLUMMERGEN 5¾ MILES. Of course, that way must lead to the road by the canal which ran by the bottom of her garden. Should she? And, then again, could she? Five and three-quarter miles. It was so like material in the old days which had never sounded so extravagant at five-eleven-three as it would have done at six shillings. But, even so, it was very far. But, again. Surely, distances between places were always measured from the center. In the same way as London always meant Hyde Park Corner. Or was it Piccadilly? She was already on what one might call the outskirts of Rye, which would, in that case, make a difference of a mile or so. And at Plummergen her garden went right down to the canal, so that she was really nearer than it. Nearer than

Plummergen, she meant. And that should make a difference. Well, not so much of a difference in a tiny village, but something. So, all in all, the distance between where she stood and where she lived should be considerably less than that given on the signpost. Shouldn't it? Encouraged, Miss Seeton fished inside her handbag. Yes, she had her little flashlight. After all, when one got to the canal it was quite straight, so presumably the road was too. A year ago, one must admit, one wouldn't have considered it, but things had changed. Or, rather, to be precise, she had. There was no question, in spite of the fact that many of the positions were strange and even embarrassing, that that book *Yoga and Younger Every Day* had made a big difference. Really she was very grateful to the advertisement which had seemed to jump at her from the newspaper: ARE YOUR KNEES STIFF? Well, they had been. And now they weren't. So she might just as well put them to good use. Besides, a brisk walk—well, perhaps not too brisk. After all, it was quite far. But a good steady walk—would help the circulation and keep her warm. Miss Seeton crossed the road and started down the short, steep slope that led to the road below. Yes, she would be perfectly all right. She had her warm coat on and, in any case, it was better than standing about because, as one had begun to realize, it was very cold.

"Are you sure, Sir George, that Miss Seeton will be on this road?"

"No."

"Oh." Arthur Treeves was puzzled. He gave the matter thought. "Wouldn't it be better then perhaps if we went somewhere she would be?"

"It would, padre, if we knew where."

"Yes. Of course, I see." Though Arthur Treeves did not. An owl swooped across the road. The vicar swung round in excitement. "Long, I think—yes, I really think long-eared, don't you?"

Sir George drove on. Hoped that little woman was all shipshape. Under cover somewhere. Cold night. And very windy.

Plummergen may be an odd five miles from Rye, but the distance was presumably judged by a crow in a hurry and, although Miss Seeton might share the crow's impatience, she had neither its sense of direction nor its wings. The road is for ground traffic with no need for haste. It is bumpy, it wanders, returns on its tracks, it meanders, until it forks sharp right over a bridge for the beginning of the canal road. The canal may be straight. The road is not. It has straight stretches, on one side the ground drops a sheer ten feet or so to the canal, on the other wherever the land rises the road takes the line of least resistance and veers toward the canal in hairpin loops. It is narrow, with no room for passing, and even a pedestrian, on the approach of a car and according to where they meet, will have to take to the grass, to the water, or climb a bank. By the time Miss Seeton had reached the bridge the light from her small flashlight was down to bulb-glow. She dropped it into her handbag. Never mind, although it had taken rather longer to get here than one had expected, it should be quite straight now. After all, one's eyes soon became accustomed to the dark and one should be able to see outlines. She must be careful to keep to the right-hand side of the road because, although the canal was only a few feet wide, the banks to it, she remembered, were very steep and one didn't want to miss one's footing. Especially since now one was out in the open it really was very windy.

On the road back from New Romney, Sergeant Ranger slowed the car almost to a stop. Anne Knight peered through the side window. No, it was a tree trunk lying near the hedge. He accelerated and changed gear. Wherever she'd got herself to he hoped Miss Seeton was all right. It was cold and windy and—he switched on the windshield wipers—it was beginning to rain.

Really, with such a strong wind, one was so very fortunate to have it behind one, helping one along. But—how tiresome—it was beginning to rain. Miss Seeton put up her umbrella. She came upon the first of the loops unexpectedly, faltered and the wind, ever helpful, caught her umbrella and sent her trotting smartly round it. Miss Seeton plowed on her way. The wind grew stronger, the rain heavier, Miss Seeton wetter. Light glowed ahead outlining another bend in the road. A car coming. Oh dear, there was no room. And they wouldn't be able to see her till too late. Where could she ...? Perforce she scrambled up the bank. Slowly the light grew stronger. Slowly a car rounded the curve. Slowly the little M.G., Nigel Colveden straining to see through the driving rain and Mel Forby trying to look through the streaming window, passed below her. Slowly the taillights dwindled.

* * *

No news. Delphick fretted. The landlord of the George and Dragon had placed his office at the superintendent's disposal and had muted the telephone bell before going to bed. Where could she have gone? Delphick was certain that his reading of the situation at the cottage had been right: that she had left before it had been ransacked. It seemed too much of a coincidence to suppose that she could have met up with the raiders later, though with her propensity for walking into and out of trouble almost anything was possible. But when was she going to walk in out of this? It was after midnight and Sir George's battalions would be returning. If any of them had had anything to report they'd have come back earlier or have phoned. Sir George's idea at best had been a worthwhile but a way-out chance. No proper search could be organized till daylight. Up to a point he felt responsible. It was he who'd drawn her into the case, though he could hardly be held to account for her antics at the post office. Why couldn't she have told someone where she was going? Then at least they … The telephone bell gave a buzz. It was Ashford. A short conversation and Delphick replaced the receiver. A burglary in the village: just what they needed to round the night off. Ashford had sent a squad car over to deal with it and they could cope. Why must thieves choose tonight of all nights, with so many people loose around the countryside—and the patrols already busy enough? Probably the reason. And with Miss Seeton missing, half the village would be certain to muddle the issue by casting her as a sort of acquisitive flitter-mouse, winging her way through their back windows, pinching heirlooms. However, it wasn't his pigeon … Yet … It matched. He jumped to his feet. Child killings, post-office raids, increase in thefts from houses and flats. He'd better check. Not worth taking the car. He headed up the Street in the punishing rain. Headlights blinded him and a car shot past, saturating his ankles as it hit a puddle. He hunched into his raincoat. People should be booked for not dipping their lights. And speed in this downpour was madness.

Headlights, dazzling, coming fast. How very reckless in weather like this. Miss Seeton jumped for the high side bank, hauled herself up, a foot slipped, she clutched, dropping her umbrella—oh, dash. She turned her head: Oh, no, eyes widened in horror, oh, no, please no. With the wind as direction finder the umbrella beamed on its target, cavorted on its way. A shout, a high-pitched scream, protesting tires braked on a slippery road, curses, another scream as the umbrella ferrule hit the windshield, splintered it, and made a hole, striking the driver on the nose and drawing blood. The car swung sideways, seemed to pause, surprised and airborne, before it tilted, dropped—a final scream—and sploshed into the canal. Dreadful—dreadful. And all her fault. Oh dear, oh dear. Miss Seeton's heart was racing, her feet were racing, pelting down the bank. Too fast. Rain was pelting down. Soaked shoes on sodden grass. The wind, still helpful, whirled her on. She tried to stop. Too late. She paddled gamely into space. She in her turn was falling, to splash beside the car in the canal.

A squad car was parked outside a house halfway up the Street. Delphick crossed over and read the name on the gate. Lilikot? Not the address he'd been given. Recognizing him, the driver made to get out but the superintendent waved him back.

"No point in both of us getting drowned. If it won't flood your carburetor or ruin the upholstery, I'll sit in a moment." He opened the passenger door and sat down with a squelch. "Why here?"

He learned that this second burglary had been reported while the Ashford inspector with a sergeant had still been making inquiries at the first house. Silver and jewelry mostly, the driver had gathered. The car number came through on the speaker: he turned up the volume. "Burglary, Glenvale House, one mile outside village on Brettenden Road. Also car stolen," the speaker told him. "Name of Farmint and v. up," it added. The driver started to open his door: Delphick stopped him.

"I'll give the inspector the glad news. And tell him that Mr. and, or, Mrs. Farmint is, or are, very upset. When we've finished here I'll probably come along to the Farmints' with you. Keep tabs on any messages for me, please."

"Certainly, sir."

Delphick got out, bolted for the shelter of Lilikot's front door, and rang the bell.

* * *

Miss Seeton struggled to her feet. Those poor, poor people in the car. She must hurry and see what she could do. At least they weren't likely to be drowned. The water barely came above her knees. But they might be unconscious. Badly injured. If she could get the car open. It proved to be unnecessary. The front and rear doors facing her swung wide. No one was in the car. Oh dear, they must have been thrown out. They might be drowning after all. One headlight still shone under water. How? she wondered fleetingly. One had always understood that water and electricity didn't mix. But at least she could see. She looked around. Was there a movement? Yes, over there, on the other side, just beyond the edge of the light. A figure emerged from the canal and scrabbled up the bank. A second figure followed: slipped, fell sideways. For an instant through the slanting rods of rain wet clothes were outlined clinging to a girl's slight figure. Long dark hair streamed. Both figures sprawled their way up, to vanish in the dark. There was a fizz. The headlight died.

Delphick quitted Lilikot with relief to accompany the Ashford inspector to the scene of the next and, he devoutly hoped, the last of the night's burglaries. However upset the Farmints might turn out to be, they could hardly prove more *v.* up than had Miss Nuttel and Mrs. Blaine. From the too, too voluble complaints, Delphick had gathered that among the list of valuables stolen the most bewailed were a cameo brooch of Miss Nuttel's, inherited from an aunt, and a too exquisite Georgian silver teapot of Mrs. Blaine's, and a too irreplaceable ruby ring set in gold, a genuine heirloom, which had belonged to Mrs. Blaine's grandmother. By the end of the too, too tiresome recital, the superintendent had felt that he not only knew too much about Mrs. Blaine but too much about her grandmother and too many other generations too.

Before going on to the Farmints' the squad car took Delphick down to the George and Dragon. Mel Forby had been dropped a few minutes earlier by Nigel Colveden. No news. It struck the superintendent that Miss Forby was looking strained and anxious. He told her there was nothing further that she could do and she would be well advised to go to bed. Mel refused, saying she would prefer to wait. Delphick shrugged: reporters were all the same, once they got their teeth into a story they never let go. As he was leaving, Anne Knight drove up with Bob. No news. He sent Anne home, brought Bob up to date on the night's activities and left him in charge of the telephone in the office. He returned to the squad car and set out for the Farmints'. No news ... Except burglaries galore. In an idiotic, backhanded way that made his concern for Miss Seeton's fate the more acute. Murder—yes. No one could stop a determined murderer; only clear up the ensuing mess. But robbery was different. Where theft was in question, especially in her own bailiwick, Miss Seeton was usually to be found in there with the best, retrieving, lashing out with her umbrella, and generally creating havoc. This time, it seemed, she wasn't. The situation was becoming very worrisome indeed.

Was it getting lighter? Or was it just that one's eyes were becoming acclimatized? No, she was right. She could see the rain now as well as hear and feel it, glinting here and there in gold. Well, there was no moon, so it had to be—yes, it could only be—the headlights of a car. Miss Seeton felt cheered. If she could attract their attention … In the faint light the realities of her predicament became apparent. She was in a deep ditch, some ten feet below the road, on a dark night, in a storm. There was no possibility that anyone in the car would be able to see her. And unlikely that they would be able to hear her against the noise of their engine. Even supposing she could make herself heard above the weather. Miss Seeton felt dashed. She would, of course, try calling out when she judged the car to be near enough, but meanwhile she'd better fend for herself while she could. She looked across at the opposite bank. Yes, that would be best. It didn't seem quite so steep. Those poor people in the car had managed it. And if they could so could she. And in any case they were sure to have gone for help. For the car that was. Naturally they could have no idea that she'd been so careless as to fall into the canal as well. At least, she reflected with satisfaction, although the accident had been entirely her fault, they hadn't appeared to be seriously hurt.

A black swan, its head gleaming in the strengthening light, glided on the water between her and the car. It nudged her. Miss Seeton gave a startled squeak and turned. Oh, really, how very fortunate. Her umbrella. Miss Seeton reached. Coyly it backed, hitting the open rear door. Something fell. Miss Seeton waded forward. She grasped her umbrella and began to close it. It resisted. She put her hand down and from below the spokes withdrew—how very odd—a ring. She opened her soggy handbag and put the ring inside for safety; thank goodness the straps were strong. You could say what you liked, but these old-fashioned bags were the best. Once you'd hooked them over your arm they stayed with you even in emergencies.

The car shifted, tilted slightly, inside it something moved. Something shining slipped, began to fall. She caught it. It couldn't be …? Aladdin's lamp? No, no, of course, a teapot. On the floor an open-mouthed sack leaned toward her. She pushed the teapot in; below it shone more silver. How very strange. Had those poor people been moving house? she wondered. But, no, because, surely, one would wrap the things in tissue. Or, at least, in newspaper. How dreadful. There was, or course, probably some explanation. But, after all, there'd been the post office and these things might, just might, be stolen. The car, subsiding, moved again; so did the sack. It clinked. Oh dear, Miss Seeton clutched at it. It was heavy. The car, as though realizing her difficulty, tilted again. The sack fell out. Miss Seeton hauled. The sack, heavier now with water, refused to budge. She couldn't leave the things. They might belong to somebody. She hauled again, she pulled and tugged and toted. Slowly the sack rose, lightening as the water drained away. She pushed it up the bank.

It wouldn't stay. She kept her shoulder under it, took her umbrella and spiked the ferrule through the top of the sack into the earth. The sack remained pinned to the bank like an outsize Christmas stocking. There, that was done.

Miss Seeton paused, feeling a little dizzy. Her teeth began to chatter with the cold. A sense of languor grew upon her; things became unreal. Bearing rich gifts of silver and of jewels … Surely so very wrong to be so very blonde. But then again, dark hair and streaming … Much more appropriate. It was all research. Trembling a little, Miss Seeton slumped and sat. The water lapped her chin. Irritated, she tried to push it away. The movement roused her. This wouldn't do. She'd heard of people falling asleep in snow, but that was no excuse for dropping off in a canal.

The light was bright, a broad swath shining high over her head on to the opposite bank, leaving her in comparative gloom. Perhaps this was the moment. She'd better try.

"Help," piped Miss Seeton.

She listened. Only the wind and the incessant beat of rain. No answering shout; but then no one, she was sure, could have heard her. Maybe if she climbed on the car and waved … She studied it. It burrowed, hood down, in the canal like a pig feeding in its trough. But the back rose high: if she could get up there … She looked for handholds. The car loomed over her. Surely it had been straighter before? She put her hand on the top of the door and pulled. The car, cooperative and friendly, tipped toward her. Quickly she let go. It swayed gently at its new angle. Oh dear, she'd been right. It had been straighter. Slowly, inevitably, it was toppling—falling on her. She must get out at once. She dug her fingers into the slimy bank and tried to raise one foot. She failed. She tried the other. Failed again. She exerted all her strength. To no purpose. Oh dear, oh dear. Both feet were stuck solid in the mud. What could she do? She—she mustn't panic. She must think and work it out. Of course—that was it. Work them out. She bent, felt under water and tried to scoop the mud from around her ankles. Quite close she heard a tinkle, then, distantly, a clank. She looked up, stared. The sack and her umbrella … But—they'd gone.

The car canted again. Miss Seeton turned her head. It was coming slowly down. Oh, please, no, please. She flung herself at the bank, stretched high and clawed. Her feet remained stuck fast. Above her the car wavered; no longer friendly, threatening now.

A slap upon one wrist, a clutch, a painful pull. The other wrist vise-gripped and dragged. She raised her head. A sullen, wet face was close to hers. Angry eyes glared through dripping lashes into hers.

The shy boy. "So kind," Miss Seeton gasped. "So sorry … A little difficult … My feet … they've stuck."

Spread-eagled down the bank, his feet dug in, he took a steady strain. Miss Seeton's arms felt they would pull from their sockets; something would have to give. It did. With a vulgar pop one foot came free. She toe-holed on the bank, then heaved and freed the other. It jerked her upward. The car, disturbed by these convulsions, sighed and, with a ripple, lay down where she had been. One by one hands let go her wrists, slid over her shoulders and along her arms, to clutch her waist. The boy wriggled backwards a few inches up the near perpendicular slope, braced himself, and waited. Miss Seeton, pulling on his strength, wormed her way up and paused. Thus, stop and go, they reached the top at last and sat there blown, in triumph.

On the road, which barely contained its width, a lorry was standing facing toward Plummergen: the headlights shone upon the sack and her umbrella.

"Oh dear—it's full of silver," said Miss Seeton. So difficult to give the facts. But only fair. It must, she realized, seem a little strange. "They left it," she explained, "when they climbed out. And you see I feel responsible because, of course, it was my fault that they were ever in. The umbrella, you know," she added to make it clear. "But in a sack like that it does seem odd and might be, don't you think, not theirs at all? But either way I feel we must take it to the police. Don't you?"

"S'right," agreed the boy.

He stood, picked up the sack, and working his way round between the lorry and the narrow shoulder, dumped it over the tailboard. Miss Seeton retrieved her umbrella and following him clambered into the cab on the driver's side and eased herself across the seat. The boy jumped in, switched on the ignition, revved, engaged the gears and, wipers clicking, drove on down the road. Beside him dripped Miss Seeton.

The police left the Farmints' little wiser than when they had arrived. They had added to the list of silver and valuables stolen, but not to their knowledge of the thief or thieves. In each case entry had been effected through a back window; the window showing signs of having been forced. In the two he had seen Delphick suspected that the scratches and splintering round the catches had been done later for effect. The windows could have been forced but the marks in both cases were so alike that they made him wonder. They had, he considered, the feeling of inside jobs or at all events of jobs that had been inspired by inside information. Little had been disturbed: the thief going straight for what he wanted. There had been no noise and, although it was possible to jimmy a window unnoticed, it was impossible to do it in silence. That three households should have failed to have heard any such sounds seemed to be carrying the burglar's luck to extremes.

The first victims had discovered their loss when the daughter of the house had gone downstairs to fetch some milk and found the kitchen window open. At Lilikot Mrs. Blain had noticed that her dressing-table drawer was disarranged and her ring missing when she was preparing for bed. The owner of Glenvale House, on hearing a car in his drive, had looked out the bedroom window in time to see his own car disappearing. Mrs. Farmint had rung the police while her husband searched the house, and, finding silver missing and his wife's jewel case gone, they had rung the police again.

The superintendent had decided and the Ashford inspector had concurred that the fact that Doris Quint was newly employed at all three houses was a pointer which could not be ignored. Although it was now nearly one o'clock, they determined to pay the Quints an immediate visit and hear what Mrs. Quint had to say. Delphick begged the use of the Farmints' telephone before setting out for Plummergen Common. Bob reported: still no news. The weather had not abated and Delphick's concern for Miss Seeton increased. Although he knew it to be virtually useless he was beginning to brood upon the possibility of calling out reserves and instituting a night search.

The lorry stopped. The boy jumped out, signing to her to stay. Miss Seeton watched. He went into a small cottage.

A light came on. A moment later a light appeared in an upstairs window. Of course. He must have gone to explain things to his wife. Such a kind boy. And so thoughtful. She peered through the windshield; through the rain. Surely—why, yes—they were just by the bridge over the canal which led up to her cottage. Barely two minutes and the boy was back. The childish figure of a girl was silhouetted in the open doorway: a hand was raised in half salute and the door closed. Miss Seeton struggled with the stiff handle on her side and climbed out. He hurried round to help her.

"You've been so very, very good," she told him. "and I'm more than grateful. But this is just near where I live. I can easily walk from here. I've got the keys to the back in my bag." She fished among the sad, soaked contents and produced them. "It would really be better, in a way, than driving up, because the noise might wake people. Whereas if I walk I can slip in unnoticed. And, after all," she looked down—things dripped and draggled; the proud hat with the bit that stuck up on top that you couldn't mistake, no longer proud and the bit, still unmistakable, hung in a sad cowlick on her brow, "I couldn't be wetter, could I?"

The faintest trace of smile. "S'right," agreed the boy.

She tried to shake his hand. He ignored her. She turned to go. He followed. Together they splashed up the lane. She unlocked the side door in the wall, went in. He followed. She held out her hand. He ignored it. With the side door closed they made their way across the garden to the kitchen. She unlocked it and prepared to say good-bye. He ignored her and went in. She followed. He switched on lights, he opened doors, looked into rooms. She made to speak. He ignored her and went upstairs. She followed. He found the bathroom, turned on taps, and gestured her toward her bedroom. Miss Seeton took a towel and laid it on the floor, stripped off her clinging clothes and dropped them onto it, picked up her nightdress and put on her dressing gown. Really, so very, very kind. The young. So truly thoughtful. She repaired to the bathroom. The boy had gone.

Relaxed in hot water—one was so grateful for Cousin Flora's immersion heater—then dried and much restored, she returned to the bedroom. Her clothes had gone.

Set out upon the towel were the contents of her handbag. Among them, secure in plastic, Mr. Geldson's second tablet. Of course. To be taken when she went to bed. Well, she would. Though she couldn't say she'd noticed any pain. But then, of course, one had been busy. She got into bed, picked up the tablet and was about to pour water from the bedside carafe when the boy came in carrying a steaming glass. He handed it. She took it by the rim. The liquid was deep amber and was hot. She popped the tablet in her mouth, she sipped and swallowed—choked. Good gracious. Very hot. And rather burning. And not nice. But—as it coursed down her—very warming. She offered back the glass. He shook his head. She sipped again; she drank. Not nice at all. But very, very comforting inside. Things were peculiar. The ceiling slanted more than usual. The bed rose up to meet it; dipped and rose again. How very fortunate that she was never seasick. Two boys leaned over her; took two glasses.

"Sho ver' kine," she muttered.

Three boys turned out three lights and left the room. She dropped back on her pillows.

Light shone behind a curtain at Saturday Stop. Doris Quint, in a dressing gown and with a towel round her head, answered the door and regarded the dripping policemen with disfavor.

"The fuzz? At this time o' night? What d'you want?"

They told her. She appeared to be shocked but maintained, rather overemphatically, that she didn't see it was any business of hers. She couldn't, she explained, ask them in since, as they could see, she weren't dressed seeing she'd just been washing her hair before getting to bed. Didn't get much time in the day what with this and that, and with her husband asleep and the boy in bed, well, they could see how it was. They had no authority to enter and she kept them standing in the downpour while she propounded her husband's breakdown, his need for sleep, the danger of disturbing him, her little brother's difficulties, her own, and how she managed she didn't really know. In length, she was voluble but uninformative.

At that the officers had to leave it, unimpressed and unconvinced. They discussed it in the car. Doris's manner and her instinctive use of the word "fuzz" suggested some knowledge of crime or criminal associates. She might have been washing her hair; then she might have been drying it after having been out in the rain, though in such weather she could have been expected to wear some form of protection. Her husband might have been asleep; or out of sight; or out. On vague suspicion alone they were in no position to insist on seeing him. The little brother, they felt, could probably be discounted as being too young. The Ashford inspector reminded Delphick that the whole Quint family were alibied for the post-office raid.

Delphick grunted. "Picnics in March."

The squad car dropped the superintendent off at the George and Dragon before returning to base. Delphick hesitated, worried and unable to settle his mind: should he turn in and contain his anxiety till morning, which was the obvious and sensible course to adopt, or should he drag out a lot of overworked men on a filthy night to scour the countryside for miles around, knowing such a move, though it might assuage his conscience, would be virtually useless until morning? Once it was light enough they could call in a helicopter which, apart from the advantage of aerial observation, could correlate the searchers and save valuable time. She might be anywhere: miles away, or close; holed up somewhere because of the storm; or even, in view of her uncanny knack for getting herself out of difficulties in the same predestined manner with which she got herself into them, asleep—tucked up in bed somewhere by a kindly good Samaritan.

He looked across at Sweetbriars. On impulse he determined to check the cottage; to assure himself there'd been no further trouble there before making a final decision. The police had arranged to leave the front door shut but unlocked as it seemed unlikely there would be another disturbance and, more particularly, in case Miss Seeton was found and they should have need of quick access without the necessity for rousing Martha Bloomer, possibly in the early hours.

The moment Delphick opened the door he sensed a change. It hadn't the feel of an empty house. Something ... yes, a smell of damp cloth. He traced it to the kitchen. Neatly laid out on chairs and table were Miss Seeton's sopping clothes. Her handbag, empty and upside down, still dripped upon the drain board beside a rinsed-out glass. In the sink stood her umbrella.

He turned, looked quickly into the other rooms, then ran upstairs. Forgetful of decorum, he flung open her bedroom door, switched on the light. He stopped and stared. Miss Seeton ignored the intrusion. Miss Seeton slept.

Near Delphick's feet the towel with its handbag medley caught his attention. He knelt down: all soaking. What had she been doing? Even she couldn't've gone swimming fully clothed. And yet … He remembered she had once fallen in a pond. That too had been at night, and but for Bob she'd have been drowned. A ring? He'd never seen her wear a ring. Perhaps her godmother's or her mother's, carried for sentimental reasons, a sort of heir- … A red stone, set in gold? A genuine heirloom? She couldn't've been—was it possible she'd been—retrieving after all? He jumped to his feet and held the ring under the light. No, not, he thought, a ruby. A carbuncle; a cabochon-cut garnet. But people did exaggerate their treasures. Particularly a type like Mrs. Blaine. He frowned and replaced the ring. He sniffed, crossed to the bed, and stooped. He thought so—whiskey. Gently he shook her shoulder. She took no notice. He shook her harder.

Dimly, in dreams, cascades of silver and of jewels floated down rivers. Black swans accompanied them. Behind them glided Cleopatra's barge bedecked with peacock feathers. The queen reclined on cushions.

"Blon'ish wrong," Miss Seeton murmured. The queen sat up. Long dark hair streamed. "Dark hair mush more 'propriate."

Delphick strained to catch the words. Blond? Dark hair? What was all this? For her own sake, and considering that ring, he couldn't let it ride. He must find out what she'd been up to.

"Wake up, Miss Seeton," he commanded. Shook her again. "Wake up. Wake up."

Upon the river bank a figure rose; majestic. It swam to midstream, huge and dominating. "You will awake," it cried. "Awake. Awake."

How very tiresome, just when one was tired. Not now, decided Miss Seeton firmly. No, really, not just now. She sat up straight. Eyes opened wide.

"Not now, O king," said Miss Seeton distinctly and relapsed into a coma.

Delphick looked at her, helpless. His palm itched to smack her. How dare she lie there in a drunken stupor, grinning all over her face when they'd all been worrying themselves sick? He looked at her. His lips began to twitch in amusement. The crumpled little face, flushed in sleep, the lips parted in a half smile. MissEss. The wretched nickname suited her somehow. Where had the silly little scrap been, getting herself soaked and sozzled? And who'd given her the whiskey? There was none in the place, as he knew from when they'd had to go over the cottage earlier. That tumbler on the drainboard. But, no—she could hardly have carried her tipple home with her in a glass through a downpour.

Delphick hurried downstairs. He telephoned to Dr. Knight. Apologized for disturbing him. He described Miss Seeton's condition as best he could, saying that he was sure there must be more to it than whiskey. She couldn't, he felt certain, be as drunk as that. Would Dr. Knight mind very much having a look at her?

Dr. Knight replied that he would mind very much indeed, considering the hour. He'd be along in five minutes.

Thankful, Delphick rang his sergeant and told him to let Ashford know Miss Seeton had been found.

Bob arrived with news: the loot from the burglaries had been recovered and the thief detained. A patrol, following instructions to question all drivers in the search for Miss Seeton, had stopped a lorry on the Brettenden Road. Not satisfied with the driver's manner, they had searched the lorry and found the missing silver and jewels in a wet sack. They were checking the items against the list now. The driver's license gave his name as Leonard Hosigg with an address near Rochester. He claimed to be working for a haulage firm in Brettenden to which the lorry belonged. His explanation was the old gag: he was on his way to Brettenden police station to hand over the stuff, which he'd found lying by the road. Questioned further, he'd clammed up and refused to say anything more. He'd been cautioned and held at Brettenden. They were not charging him till the inventory of the stolen valuables was complete. The local force, Bob told his superior, was cock-a-hoop. The burglaries solved within two hours, at least one of the post-office raiders under lock and key, and no danger now to the Goffer girl, though the watch on her was being maintained for tonight until it was called off officially.

Delphick paced the sitting room, then went to the telephone and rang Ashford headquarters. Was the inventory of the Plummergen robberies completed yet? One moment, while they checked with Brettenden… . It was. Was there a ring missing? One moment… . Yes, there was, but after all, with an open sack and things just chucked in anyhow it was a wonder more of the stuff hadn't fallen out. Pretty good going to've only lost one small ring and even that would probably be found either wedged somewhere in the lorry or else along the route. The superintendent asked for Chief Detective Inspector Brinton's home number. He rang it. The chief inspector was not pleased. Delphick suggested that it might be wise not to charge the Hosigg boy till further inquiries had been made. Brinton, roused from sleep at half past one and knowing only half the facts, nearly blew his top. What for God's sake did the

Oracle want? To catch a chummie redhanded, then not charge him? Further inquiries into what? All right, they'd solved the Oracle's cases for him, hadn't they? All right, he'd got his girl friend back again, hadn't he? So all right, everything was hunky-dory. What more did he want? For once they'd got a nice straight case, and Miss Seeton hadn't stirred it up with her umbrella and pinched the oodle back herself.

Delphick was apologetic. "That's the trouble, Chris. I can't be certain yet, but I think there's a faint possibility she did. She's got a ring here that might be the one that's missing."

"What's she say about it?"

"That's just it. She can't. I'll ask her in the morning."

"The morning?" demanded Brinton. "Why not now?"

"I can't, Chris. She's asleep."

"All right, so she's asleep; so all right, wake her up. Do we all have to stop for tea because the lady's having a kip?"

Delphick began to appreciate Miss Seeton's occasional difficulty in explaining things. "It's not quite as easy as that, Chris. You see she's er—well, drunk."

"She's what?" barked Brinton.

"Yes," added Delphick hurriedly. "I've called the doctor."

"All right, all right, she's drunk; and so all right, you've called the doctor. I'll tell my old woman, next time I've had a drop, to quit narking and call the vet." A gusty sigh came down the telephone. "I'll ride along, Oracle, and get on to Brettenden and tell them to hold things over till the morning. And for the Lord's sake, when your lady comes back from her holiday, let's have it penny-plain, not tuppence-colored." He rang off.

The sergeant was popeyed. "You mean Miss Seeton's squiffed, sir? She couldn't be. I mean she wouldn't be. I mean ..."

Delphick sounded tired. "I get your meaning, Bob, but it doesn't alter facts. She's blotto."

"I'm sure she wouldn't touch it, sir. And anyway, where would she get hold of it?"

"That's just the point, Bob. If we knew that, we'd know a great deal more than we do."

Delphick was reaching for the telephone again when Dr. Knight arrived. Before following him upstairs he instructed Bob to get on to Brettenden and find out if Hosigg had any whiskey on him or any in the lorry, then to have a look at Miss Seeton's clothes in the kitchen and to smell the rinsed tumbler on the drainboard to see if there was any trace of whiskey there.

Dr. Knight wasted little time in the bedroom and came downstairs in high good humor. The police, he suggested, might be well advised to take elementary courses in nursing. Nothing difficult; just beginners' stuff. Then possibly they might be able to recognize such very simple facts as when a lady had quite obviously been to a dentist and had a tooth out, had been given a sedative—one of the barbiturates, he should say—then gone and taken it with spirits, which had knocked her out. Then, instead of mauling her about and trying to indulge in chatty conversation, they might have wit enough to leave her alone and let her sleep it off. "And don't," he added at the front door, "try waking her with early-morning tea at eight o'clock. If you do, you'll have her half doped all day and with a splitting headache. Wait till she wakes on her own—about midday probably from the look of it." He glanced at his watch. "Good morning to you." He nodded and departed.

Bob reported that Brettenden said there was a half-empty flask of whiskey in Hosigg's overcoat pocket. Delphick expressed satisfaction and the two officers went up to the bedroom for a final look at Miss Seeton and a detailed examination of the sad little array of objects on the towel. They knelt down and sorted through the things carefully, but nothing appeared unusual except the ring—and the fact that everything was wet.

"Playing crap, boys?" inquired Mel from the doorway. "Mind if I sit in and have a throw?"

Bob was embarrassed, Delphick wild. He got up slowly. In deference to Miss Seeton he kept his voice quiet.

"And so we have the press. Charming. Trespass, breaking and entering, obstructing the police in the execution of their duties …"

"Obstructing nothing," flashed Mel. "If you two clowns want to shoot crap in a lady's bedroom at two A.M., that's all right by me, I'll not stop you. I've not broken a thing and as for trespass," she turned to the bed, "well, I guess you could call me a friend of the corpse. What gives?"

Without answering, Delphick crossed to the door, ushered Mel out and down the stairs. Bob switched off the light, closed the door and followed them.

In the sitting room, Mel sat relaxed, Delphick stood, Bob hovered.

"Perhaps you'd be kind enough," suggested the superintendent, "to explain this intrusion even if you can't excuse the impertinence."

"Why, sure," said Mel ironically. "Just a friendly call. You know, human interest stuff."

"Quite. For human interest I suggest we read muckraking. Has it never occurred to you the damage you can do by hounding people to get a story? Prying into their lives to get a story? Twisting facts and making suggestions just this side of libel, and all to get a story? Oh, no—nothing's sacred in the name of news and everything's excused, to get a story."

"My, my," said Mel in admiration. "Sir Galahad himself." She sat forward in her chair. Her expression hardened. "You'd like it then," she snapped, "that I should make it front-page stuff? *Police Orgy in Battling Brolly's Bedroom. Miss Seeton missing half the night. Big police hunt. Three burglaries reported. Miss Seeton's whereabouts still unknown. Is she involved? Two police officers found in Miss Seeton's bedroom after 2 A.M. with Miss Seeton asleep in bed and a strong smell of whiskey.*

Delphick looked grim. "You'll find, Miss Forby, that the police have means of making things difficult for reporters when they wish; so difficult that in the long run editors sometimes find it more expedient to employ someone else, if they want to get their facts without undue delay."

"Threats yet, or I'm a Dutchwoman. And has it occurred to you," asked Mel, "you half-baked crusader, that I know about you fetching Miss S to the Lewisham morgue to draw a stiff? All in the name of chivalry, I guess. What's more, I've seen the drawing of this Goffer child." Delphick's head jerked up. "That shakes you, huh? Know, near enough, what brings you here, and near enough what gives in all directions. And have I spilled it? No, I've played along. Miss S is news—I can't help that—but have I said so? No, I've plugged the Brolly angle so they'll forget the name. Sure, I'm following a story—on orders. Sure, I hope to make a scoop. But not at her expense, you dope. What d'you think I am? A scandal sheet?"

Delphick spread his hands, then sat down. "Miss Forby, I apologize …" he began.

"If you mean that, make it Mel."

"Right. I'm sorry, Mel."

"So, let's start over. I'll send in nothing without you oversee it and we all protect little old Innocence upstairs. You know," Mel shook her head in wonder, "somehow she gets me."

Their differences resolved and a firm foundation established, Delphick made it clear that, although it would be a disciplinary offense for him to give any information whatever to the press, in view of the fact that Mel was a friend of Miss Seeton's, he had no authority to throw her out of the house. If she chose to sit there while he discussed with his sergeant what they knew of the night's events he was powerless to prevent her.

Finally, Mel took cushions and seats from the chairs, found a rug and made a bed for Bob on the floor, the sofa being far too short. They had agreed that under no circumstances should Miss Seeton be left alone in the cottage. Delphick would have to go over to Ashford early and pacify the chief inspector. Mel would look in at Sweetbriars during the morning and, when Miss Seeton woke, would ask her if she minded going to Ashford to make a statement. They wrote a brief note to Martha Bloomer to acquaint her with the situation so that she wouldn't worry or disturb Miss Seeton.

Mel Forby and the superintendent, huddled amicably under her inadequate umbrella, set off to drop the note and return to the George and Dragon.

Bob settled down philosophically to a few hours of wakeful discomfort.

Miss Seeton slept.

Chapter 7

Miss seeton woke. She felt relaxed and comfortable; disinclined for movement. Gently the happenings of the night returned to her. Really, Mr. Geldson was very clever. No trouble with her mouth at all… . Come, this wouldn't do. She mustn't lie about.

She got up, had a bath, went back to the bedroom, and laid out fresh clothes. She wondered for a moment where her wet things were. Well, time enough for that. She made the bed. How very odd. The mattress wasn't hers. She looked around. The cushion on the easy chair was different. Where had they come from? Perhaps Martha had started a spring clean; they must be hers, lent while her own were being seen to. She'd ask her. She began to dress—stopped, restless. Last night … Her hands began to flutter. She opened a dressing-table drawer, took a drawing block and pencils. Last night … Yes, that was it, she'd put it down. She'd set down everything that happened while it was clear in her mind. Happily she squatted and plunged into work.

When she had finished she laid the block aside, her mind and hands at peace. Really, she must get dressed. She felt lethargic and, as she began to get to her feet, perhaps a little stiff. She'd probably be wise to—what was it the games mistress always called it? Ah, yes, of course—to give herself a workout. Before making herself some toast and tea she'd do her exercises.

Mel Forby opened the front door quietly, crept upstairs, carefully lifted the latch of the bedroom door and looked in. On the floor, in stockings, bloomers, and a jumper knelt Miss Seeton. Knees together, feet apart, she sat between them: overarm and underarm her hands were clasped behind her back. Her eyes were closed, her breath was held, her lips moved as she counted. Mel gaped.

"Well, fry me for supper," she exclaimed. "Miss S, what are you doing?"

Miss Seeton's eyes opened. She turned her head slightly. Four … Five … How very awkward. One mustn't let go one's breath or lose one's count. But then, again, one must, of course, reply. From counting, breath control, and strain, her voice came strangled.

"Cow-Face," said Miss Seeton.

Well, ask a personal question, and—wow!—did you get a personal answer. Softly Mel closed the door, and went downstairs. In the kitchen she gathered up Miss Seeton's still damp outer clothes and tied them in a bundle for the cleaners. She put the kettle on, cut the bread, took butter from the fridge, found marmalade, and laid for breakfast. She went through to the sitting room. The sergeant, who had returned to the inn when daylight came, had left it neat and tidy. She rang him. Miss Seeton was awake, she told him, but not yet fully dressed or fed. Give them, say, half an hour. She put the receiver back. The telephone bell rang: the Colvedens. The telephone bell rang: Miss Treeves. The telephone bell rang:

Anne Knight. The telephone bell rang: the Oracle. Mel coped with all. From the little table in the passage she collected the post and put it on Miss Seeton's plate. She couldn't fail to notice and to be intrigued by an official-looking envelope inscribed: *MissEss, Sweetbriars, Plummergen, Kent.*

Mel let Miss Seeton have her meal in peace, contained her curiosity, and forebore to question her about the previous night. The meal finished, she cleared the table and washed up, refusing Miss Seeton's help. She warned her of Bob's imminent arrival and the impending jaunt to Ashford. Miss Seeton was resigned. She deplored, but acknowledged, the necessity. At least she could hand over that ring which worried her. And then the whole affair could be forgotten. She tackled her post. She looked at the official envelope a moment, puzzled. Then her expression lightened, she smiled and opened it. It contained a check and a note, Mel observed from her position at the sink. Miss Seeton read the note, frowned, and shook her head. She looked at the check, looked closer, and gave a small "Oh" of dismay. The note was most kind, but quite undeserved. In it Delphick explained that he felt, and Sir Hubert Everleigh agreed, that the Effie Goffer drawing formed a part of their case and so, with her permission, they were keeping it and had made the check for double the amount to include both sketches. But the check … Oh dear. Apart from its generosity … She looked at it again. Yes, she'd been right. It was signed *on behalf of the Reciever for the Metropolitan Police District.* Really, how dreadful. One knew, of course, that things were bad. And one had read that the police were underpaid. But to have the receiver in … One had had no idea that things were as bad as that. One would not, of course, cash the check; but should she, she wondered, send a small donation? Miss Seeton was distressed.

"What's biting you, honey?" inquired Mel.

Oh. Now that was very difficult. Should one mention it? Perhaps the police preferred to keep it quiet. But then, again, one understood that the press knew everything and was always very careful what it said. Certainly she couldn't ask the superintendent—so embarrassing—and that nice sergeant, she felt, might not quite understand. Whereas Miss Forby—well, Mel … She looked at her. Began to study her. The eye makeup: so very much improved. Those hard, flat planes, the generous mouth, the high and wide-set cheekbones—so interesting—leading to slight hollows which threw into relief the broad brow; all softened, brought together by those quite, quite lovely eyes. Now—where was she? Ah, yes. Mel could probably advise her. She showed the check to her; described her problem. Mel tried, tried hard, to play it straight and then collapsed.

"No one but you-hoo-hoo," she hooted, "could think they'd got the bums in at the Yard." She whooped again in glee.

Miss Seeton smiled, uncertain. When Mel had made it plain that the receiver was not the official one, but an august personage in control of all financial dealings for the London force, Miss Seeton was relieved.

"Why the MissEss?" asked Mel.

"But, surely, they have to. They all do nowadays. Officially, that is."

"Do what?" Mel queried.

"Address each other by initials. At one time there was only C.O.D.; or C.P. if you wanted something moved. But now there are so many, it's become involved. H.P., which is a way of buying things—so very rash—or then, again, you buy it as a sauce. People, too," Miss Seeton pointed out, "with P.M.'s, M.P.'s, G.P.'s and J.P.'s. You see it everywhere. Naturally one understands that in my case the initial wouldn't do. M.S., you see, might stand for manuscript and lead to muddles. Evidently they compromised; so very wise."

A knock at the front door. That would be Bob. Mel went to see. It was a girl. Could she see the lady? Mel led her to the kitchen. The girl ran to Miss Seeton, knelt; words spilled from her.

"Please, please, miss, they took him, won't you help, Len never did it, no, never, you know that, but he'll not say anything, I know he won't, he can't, you see, because of me."

Miss Seeton took her hands. The shy boy's wife. She smiled at the tear-stained face. "Come now, we mustn't cry. Who's taken—Len, you said?—and why?"

"The cops, because they say he's pinched them things last night, but he wouldn't, you know that."

Miss Seeton was indignant. "Of course he wouldn't. Quite ridiculous. What makes them think he did? Why won't he say? And why because of you?"

"I'm under age, you see. We'd not a right to marry. That's why we came here. Len's still on appro, you see, because of a bit of bother at my home."

"Bother? I see." Miss Seeton nodded. "I think perhaps you'd better tell me exactly what did happen at your home."

"Well, it's my stepdad really, mum's silly, you see, and him he tried it on with Rosie, that's my sister, and like a fool I told Len, and then he tried it on with me and Len he was that wild he bashed him one and knocked him down the stairs. Bust three ribs. They brought it in assault, that's why Len's still on appro. Len he said I weren't to stay so we got a license and we quit but of course we haven't got the right, not in the law, not without mum's say-so me being a minor. Well, so's Len for that, that's why he got this driving job and we come down here to sort of hide, you see. But nothing wrong."

"Of course not," Miss Seeton said. "Len was right. Quite right. It was your stepfather who should have been charged. His behavior was quite dreadful. They should have realized that."

The girl looked hopeless. "They didn't know."

"Why not?"

"Len wouldn't have it. I wanted to speak up but he said no. There's mum, you see, and Rosie, then the neighbors, you know what people are, he wouldn't have me mixed up with things like that with people speaking ill. Unprovoked, they called it, but Len's got a good character and never did a thing before so they put him on appro." The girl gave a wan smile. "I suppose he was lucky really."

Miss Seeton patted her hands. "Now, now, stop worrying. This is all nonsense. Len was with me last night and very, very kind."

Mel was entranced. A new Miss S. The schoolmarm bolstering a kid in trouble. And last night's story spilling or she missed her guess.

"I know," answered the girl simply. "He popped in late and got some whiskey, said he was afraid you'd catch your death. Wet as a herring he said you was."

The sergeant, who had been waiting in the car, finally knocked. Receiving no answer and hearing voices, he'd come to the kitchen and was standing unnoticed in the doorway, spellbound.

"I was," agreed Miss Seeton. "He got me out of the canal and got the sack on the road. The kindest boy. And thoughtful."

Her hands moved, traced the air. "I put it all down on paper this morning when I woke, while it was still fresh. We'd settled he was to take it to the police. The sack I mean. I'm afraid I was a bit tired," she apologized. "He took me home and ..." She stopped nonplused. "I'm not very clear what happened after that."

Bob coughed. Startled, they turned. "If you're ready, ma'am?"

"Of course." Miss Seeton got up. "I'm so sorry, I forgot. I'll get a hat and coat."

"Perhaps, Miss Seeton," Bob suggested, "if you wouldn't mind bringing what you put down about last night, it might save time and make things easier."

Miss Seeton was dubious. "I don't think that would help."

"Oh, please, miss," said the girl.

"Go on, Miss S," encouraged Mel, "give 'em the works." Doubtful, Miss Seeton went upstairs.

"Where you taking her?" the girl demanded.

"To Ashford," Bob replied. "To make a statement."

"And she'll clear Len?" The girl's eyes shone. "Please may I come?"

"You're Mrs. Hosigg?"

"Of course. Can't I come? I've got a right; I know what happened too, Len told me."

Bob was uncertain; Mel determined. "We're all going," she informed the girl.

"No, not you, Miss Forby."

"Sure, me. You try to keep me out of this I'll have your hide for knickknacks."

Bob, knowing that he would not win, succumbed and set out with misgivings and his female freight.

Chief Detective Inspector Brinton was in a temper. The Ashford Choppers had struck again. A dance hall in Brettenden had been the scene of their foray and they had left the place a shambles. They had also left five people injured and two of the injuries were serious. One of his own men of the uniformed branch had attended the dance as a private individual. When the ruckus had started this officer had weighed in on the side of law and order. Three of the Choppers had tackled him and two had held him down while the third had belabored him about the head with a bicycle chain. He was now in Ashford hospital with brain damage and his condition was said to be critical. In court that morning the Choppers' counsel had rehearsed the theme of how his clients' youthful high spirits were misunderstood, their friendly overtures misconstrued, their wish to fraternize resented. As for his clients being armed with knives, knuckle-dusters, bicycle chains, and coshes, this was a more—a most—serious misunderstanding. His clients, he protested, had never carried—never would carry—weapons of offense. And of the youth who had been arrested with a bicycle chain wrapped round his fist before he could get rid of it, he drew a moving picture of a stainless boy examining in horror a deadly device that had been used—it went without saying—exclusively by the other side. His eloquence had so prevailed that the magistrate had once again, as always, let the boys off with a caution and a disciplinary fine of five shillings per head for any damage they had caused. Brinton's anger had left him prepared to lay the blame for all local trouble on the Choppers' shoulders and the fact that Len Hosigg had appeared upon the scene to befog the issue infuriated him. He had failed to find any connection between Hosigg and the Ashford gang; but at least the Hosigg case was cut and dried. Now to cap his morning Delphick was casting doubts and asking him to hold his hand.

"You can't get away from it. Oracle, the boy's got form. Known to be violent, ducked his probation, skipped with a minor, and gone into hiding; in fact, he's done his nut." The chief inspector put the report from the Rochester Division back on his desk. "And now we nab him with the oodle before he has time to flog it. What more d'you want? It's open and shut."

Delphick roamed the office. "Let's keep it open, Chris, until we've seen Miss Seeton." Brinton groaned. "Granted all you say, it still feels wrong. And how do you explain the whiskey and the ring?"

"Don't have to. You said yourself the ring's a garnet. The pinched one's a ruby. And as for the whiskey, who's to say the lady's not a secret toper; some of your don't-touch-me misses can swig it with the best, a bottle in every shoe, you get it all the time."

A knock. Bob entered looking sheepish. "I've brought Miss Seeton, Mrs. Hosigg, and Miss Forby, sir."

"What d'you take this for," demanded Brinton, "the women's hostel?" Delphick merely looked.

"I couldn't help it, sir," said Bob, "they would insist on coming and … they came."

"Well, ask Miss Seeton to come up. With regard to the Hosigg girl it's just as well, we'll need to see her. And you can tell Miss Forby from me," Delphick's eyes danced, "that she can stay downstairs. And not to try her luck, or me, too far."

Bob returned with Miss Seeton and a large envelope. The formalities observed, he put Miss Seeton in a chair and laid the envelope with pride on Brinton's desk.

"What's this?"

"A statement from Miss Seeton, sir." Miss Seeton opened her mouth to protest.

"You took this down, Sergeant?"

"No, sir, I haven't seen it, but Miss Seeton told me—well, Miss Forby said—well, actually I overheard Miss Seeton say she'd put down everything about last night this morning, so I asked her if she'd mind. I thought it would save time, sir." He retired to a chair with notebook and pen.

Delphick moved round behind the desk as Brinton opened the envelope and took out a sheet of paper. There was a silence while the chief inspector struggled with his feelings.

"You said you hadn't read this, Sergeant?"

"No, sir."

"Well, come and read it now."

With a sinking feeling—something was off—Bob went to the desk and looked at the paper. A cartoon of "The Knight's Vigil." In profile, in armor, the young knight knelt before an altar at his orisons. The clubbed hair framed a sullen face transformed. The hands joined in prayer held, not a sword, but one madonna lily on which the shining eye was fixed in ecstasy. Bob sighed. He should've known it'd be off. Way off.

"I said I was afraid it wouldn't help," ventured Miss Seeton as Bob went back to his chair.

Delphick smiled at her. "I'm not so sure. Is this young Hosigg?"

"Yes."

"That's your impression of him?"

"Yes."

"In short," still smiling, Delphick pointed to the drawing, "this sums up from your point of view everything of importance that took place last night."

Miss Seeton looked at him gratefully. "Well, yes. You see …" She told them of her rescue. Then gave the girl's account of why they'd come to Plummergen.

Delphick reached for the telephone, got through to Rochester, and left a message for Hosigg's probation officer, outlining the story and asking him to check; to try breaking down Hosigg's sister-in-law, a girl called Rosie. Would they ring him back? Miss Seeton was pleased. Those poor children. This should help to put things right. Delphick looked at the sketch again.

"Tell me. Why the lily?"

Miss Seeton frowned, surprised. "Lily? Is there? Oh, yes," remembering, "I think I felt it seemed more right somehow."

Delphick frowned in turn and thought. "What's his wife's name?" he asked.

"I'm sorry," said Miss Seeton, "I don't know. I never thought to ask."

"I can tell you that." Brinton flipped over some papers. "Leonard Hosigg: wife, Lil Hosigg," he read out. "Born Lily Smale." He looked at Miss Seeton; for the first time really looked at her.

Miss Seeton opened her handbag and produced the ring. "This was the ring that dropped out of the sack. Before the teapot. It caught in my umbrella. So fortunate. It might have fallen in the water. I didn't like to put it back for fear it would get lost."

Brinton read from a list. "A valuable ruby ring belonging to a Mrs. Blaine: reported stolen, not recovered." He eyed her severely. "You suggest this would be it then?"

Miss Seeton was uncertain. "But this is a garnet. At least I think so. Oh—" as she realized, "oh, I see. Perhaps it would be kinder just to give it back and not say anything."

The chief inspector stared at her, then grinned. "Like her Georgian silver teapot which is modern stuff and plated? And Miss Nuttel's cameo brooch in gold, turned pinchbeck overnight?"

Miss Seeton smiled back at him. "It's very tempting sometimes, Chief Inspector, to imagine one's things to be a little better than they really are."

"Tell me, Miss Seeton," Delphick took over, "the car that went into the canal—a car stolen from a Mr. and Mrs. Farmint, incidentally, where the last of the robberies took place—did you see what happened? Although some of the windshield splintering probably occurred when it fell, the lab reports that there's a hole which could have been caused by a shot."

Miss Seeton flushed. "No, that, I fear, was me." Brinton looked up sharply. "Or, rather, my umbrella," she amended. "I dropped it when I slipped. And with that wind, so very strong, it hit the car. Dreadful. They might have both been killed."

"Pity they weren't," said Brinton.

"You saw them?" Delphick asked.

"Oh, yes." Bob sat up, pen poised. "Just for a moment, that is, when I was in the water too, next to the car. They were climbing out the other side. Of the canal I mean. I couldn't see them well because, you see, they had their backs to me and were beyond the light." Bob relaxed. "The light from the car's lamp, that is. I mean, of course, before it fizzed and then went out." Why, wondered Bob, couldn't she talk like other people? The Oracle understood her and even old Brimstone seemed to be keeping up, but say what you like, police statements had this to be said for them; they were clear. He tried one on for size: I was proceeding under water along the canal in an easterly direction when I encountered a fizz. A chuckle escaped him. Delphick frowned. Miss Seeton continued: "But, just before it fizzed, she slipped and fell into the light. He had to grab her."

"She?" demanded Delphick. "You're certain it was a she?"

"Oh, yes. Long hair."

"It couldn't have been a long-haired boy?"

"Oh, no. No, quite impossible. Her clothes were wet and clinging. Unmistakable."

"Just been washing my hair," echoed a voice in Delphick's brain, "don't get much time in the day what with this and that." Before he was through he'd bust that picnic alibi or bust himself. He took from his pocket an old envelope on which he'd made some notes. "You spoke—forgive me, Miss Seeton, this was later when you were, er, asleep—of 'blonde being wrong.' Had that any bearing, do you know?"

Miss Seeton thought, then brightened. "Oh, no. That was the Queen of Saba. It struck me as wrong. Unless, of course, she was like Cleopatra. Greek, you know. It's all research," she added by way of explanation.

Even Delphick was fazed. "Saba?"

"Yes. You see, I went to *Sheba* because of the tea. So difficult to drink. With one's mouth, that was."

Light dawned. "Oh, of course, the film *Sheba*. Yes, I see." He referred to the envelope. "The other thing you said was 'dark hair more appropriate.'"

Miss Seeton considered. "I imagine that that might have been the girl. The girl who slipped in climbing out. Her hair was long and dark. Although, of course, it could have been the light. Or lack of it I mean."

There was nothing more of use that Miss Seeton could tell them. A call came through from Rochester. The Smale girl had come clean and, pressed, her mother backed her up. The stepfather had been brought in: under questioning and faced with his wife's defection, he had admitted the truth. He appeared to be more concerned about a charge of perjury than troubled over proceedings for attempted rape: what were stepdaughters for? The Hosigg boy was in the clear and the whole case was to be reviewed. There was no need now to see his wife. Brinton rang Brettenden and gave orders to let young Hosigg go. Goodbyes were said and Bob escorted Miss Seeton down, with instructions to return to Plummergen via Brettenden with his seraglio, picking up Len Hosigg on the way.

When the door was closed, the chief inspector laughed. "So that's your Miss Seeton, Oracle. All right, I'm sold. I'll buy her. But not too often; and can't you keep her out of crime? Well, there was this car, you see," he mimicked, "and it was in my way if you understand me so I gave it a swipe with me brolly that is and it ends up in the dike. And then of course I has to jump in too if you take my meaning just to see what's going on in a manner of speaking." He guffawed, then sobered. "All right, it's all very pretty and everything's cozy and she's got the oodle back for us as per usual. But you realize, Oracle, it doesn't mean the Hosigg lad's out of it. He may be a knight in shining armor, I'm not saying he isn't, and he may have it all over your market gardeners when it comes to growing lilies, but it doesn't say he didn't do the job, and when she pitched him in the drink, climbed out, went back and got his lorry, drove round, and pinched the stuff again."

"And the girl with him?" asked Delphick.

"His wife, of course. Once they've climbed out she scarpers home while he goes round to have a second bash."

"It hardly squares with his behavior afterwards. Why get Miss Seeton out? Why not leave her there? Why waste his time? Why take her home? Why give her whiskey? Why lay out her clothes to dry? Because he did, you know, Chris. That young man took a lot of trouble."

"All right, so I'll agree it isn't likely. The Hosiggs're out, the Quints're out. We start again from scratch, and of the runners left the odds are in favor of the Ashford lot. You'll find I'm right, Oracle, this doesn't have to be fancy; there's nothing to say that any of this is mixed up with child murder—nothing except that blasted drawing. I'd say that your Miss Seeton's got you and the A.C. chasing your tails. Let's look at what we've got: local jobs; and local chummies who'd fit the jobs. Why complicate it?"

The superintendent shrugged. "You may be right, Chris. I know it sounds reasonable, but ..."

"But you don't buy it."

The other shook his head. "I can't afford to. This killing of small children ..." He grimaced. "Oh, I'll admit there's always been the odd case, but it's suddenly spiraled—over fifty percent increase in the past two years." He shook his head. "What's got into people? And now that we've found this one series that's got a definite pattern I must stick with it, Chris, and follow it through; there's too much at stake. I know that any headline crime's liable to be copied but you don't get a carbon as accurate as that post-office raid, except once in a blue moon. Somewhere down here," Delphick frowned, "there's someone who's insane and somehow I've got to find him."

"Well," suggested Brinton, "take your pick of the Choppers. They're a bunch of halfwits if you like."

The superintendent continued unheeding. "Somewhere, somehow, a cog has slipped and someone's brain is out of gear. It's as though you were faced with a line of cars and are told that in one of them the clutch is slipping. How—without driving the cars yourself or stripping down the gears in all of them—do you make a guess as to which it is? On looks alone the Quint girl would be my fancy. Cheaply pretty, I suppose, but a bad forehead and an underhung jaw. Cunning, yes. But stable mentally? I doubt it. Wish to God I could find out something about them: background, parentage; there might be a pointer; but every line we've tried's drawn a blank."

Brinton closed the file in front of him and laid it to one side. "So, all right, Oracle, I'll leave the mental push-ups to you. We'll work it sides to middle. I'll give the Choppers a going-over and see if a couple of the little hatchets haven't sharpened themselves up. You play the psycho angle and maybe somewhere our lines'll cross."

Delphick began to pace again. "The Quints, Chris. It all hangs on the alibi. If we could find some way round that …"

Since they were going into Brettenden, she might as well go to the bank and get it over, Miss Seeton decided. That was if the sergeant didn't mind waiting. It wouldn't take more than a minute or two. She would naturally have preferred to send the check by mail, but in this case she would need to speak with the manager and explain about its being made out to her initials. Or, rather, not to her initials, which were, of course, E.D. for Emily Dorothea, but to MissEss which, when you came to think of it, was what Mel always called her. Quite natural. Newspapers and officials always did. Use initials, she meant. The manager must have met many cases like it and would understand. Certainly she would not attempt to explain to that young man. So supercilious. Of course young was relative, he must be over thirty, she supposed. Still young, she felt, to be a head cashier. She always tried, when she was in the bank, to see his colleague, but nearly always failed. Of course one knew that one's account was very small. Quite unimportant. It made one feel one should apologize for taking up their time. But the head cashier was so superior, with such a bored manner, that it was embarrassing, and usually she managed things by post.

At the bank the sergeant dropped Miss Seeton, who refused to be picked up, saying that she would walk down and join them. He took Lil Hosigg to the police station. Mel strung along. News-wise she was well in. The Brolly angle was going over fine. It had caught the public fancy, taking the spotlight off Miss S and giving the Pieces of Peace the attraction of a strip cartoon in narrative. She was on the inside track of a top news story and, provided she played it straight with the Oracle, was bound to scoop. Meanwhile these Hosigg kids were good for a bit on the side. Sound sob-sister stuff. It wouldn't hurt them any and like it or not they'd make a para or so when his case came up again.

It would happen: the assistant wasn't there. He must be out at lunch. That left her no choice: it would have to be the chief cashier. Or could she ignore him and only see the manager?

No, really, this was ridiculous; she was behaving stupidly. There was no necessity to explain to him and she would not, Miss Seeton decided, be intimidated. She would look him straight in the eye, smile, hand in the check, and ask to see the manager. She took a breath, braced herself, marched to the counter, and wrote a slip; then deflated as she fumbled in her bag. Now where had she put the check? Ah, here it was. Still fired with resolution, she drew herself up, looked the man straight in the eye … How curious. One had never looked at him before. Not, that was to say, looked. The eyes. Most unusual for such a light blue to be so brilliant. Piercing, perhaps, would be a better word. And with those flattened cheekbones and that fold of skin over the eye … After all, one associated the epicanthic fold with the rounder face of Asiatics—and, of course, with dark eyes and dark, straight hair. But to meet an external epicanthus in conjunction with light eyes was unusual—possibly therefore exaggerated their brilliance. Also, with a longish face, and that particular setting, one wouldn't have expected it to be fair and wavy. The hair, that was. Curious. And interesting … Miss Seeton passed him the check without a word of explanation, smiled at him, and said:

"I think I'd better see the manager." She went her way to knock at the inner sanctum.

The cashier watched her, narrow-eyed. Slowly he expelled the breath he'd been holding.

This was it. What passed in the cashier for a conscience began to talk to him. After years of inactivity his conscience, rudely awakened by a shock, not only talked to him, it took the floor, was voluble. If you took money, his conscience pointed out, that was not yours to take, you also took a risk and if you took risks, it went on to explain, you took the consequences. You might decide, imagine, or conclude that you were the master of your fate, that you would decide the how and when of what you did, and why. But there were things that people called externals, the unforeseen events or persons which might crop up in an unguarded moment and in cropping might, if you were not flexible and prepared for all eventualities, quite literally crop you. But in this instance, the cashier reasoned, he'd done exactly that. He had so reasoned, so foreseen, and so prepared himself.

So they'd rumbled him. And that it should be her who'd cottoned to it of all people. He was still tense but his mind was steadying now from the tailspin she'd sent him into—now that he realized he'd got a chance. For a moment he'd thought it was all up. But now … He glanced through the window. No sign of a police car in the street. No sign of watchers; but then there wouldn't be, not if they knew their job. They might be waiting for him—he'd just have to risk it. Yes, he had a chance. A chance given him by that silly old mare when she gave herself away, and in doing so had given him his *cave*. To be found out was bound to happen sometime, that he'd always known, but he'd expected to be able to judge the moment, before an audit, and to be well away before they pounced. But that dried-up old prune … To've been a police stoolie all this time—how the hell could he have guessed? The police were getting pretty fly, using old trouts like that. He'd never've suspected her, not in a hundred years. Lucky for him she couldn't resist a bit of show-off. Mouselike as a rule when she did come in, but like a mouse she'd been burrowing underground, checking on him. But now she was onto him—like a full-sized cat, puffing herself up, waving her police checks under his nose; with her code name on them too, silly old fool, then leering at him; so full of herself she couldn't hide it. And then—prissy as could be—"I'd better see the manager." She better had. Better still that she'd tipped him off, and as from now neither the manager nor she would catch a glimpse of him. Deliberately, with no appearance of haste, he took the bundles of paper money allotted to him and pushed them inside his shirt. Pin money. He'd stash this little lot, pro tem, in Ashford with Maryse. Until he was sure they'd got no record of the numbers and he'd had time to see how things were jumping. With Maryse ... His heartbeat quickened. With Maryse. Maryse: the mere thought of her stimulated him; made the game worthwhile. He'd nip round to the car park and drive his old car into the wood behind his house just outside Brettenden—the house that that old cat could have no idea of, not with all her burrowing. Slip in unnoticed across the garden, dye his hair, put on his mustache, put in his contact lenses, take the Rover from the garage, drive to the other side of the Dover motorway, and leave it near the quarry. He'd have to walk back to Brettenden; that was a sweat but he'd plenty of time. Daren't go back to his Ashford digs—too dangerous; the police were welcome to anything they found there. Collect the old car from the wood as soon as it was dusk. With muddied number plates it'd be safe enough. Leave it near the top of the quarry in the undergrowth. Then back to the Rover, to Ashford, to Maryse. He'd stay there with her at her flat till it was time to carry out the main part of his plan. His jacket was tight to button over his money-padded shirt. He left it open; turned to the typist, busy at the back.

"Hold the fort, ducks. Shan't be a tick."

"… *and unsecured loans. We regret that in the circumstances we cannot* …" She stopped, surprised. Looked up to ask him … He was gone.

Miss Seeton walked to the police station. The manager had been very understanding and just a little—could it be?—impressed. He'd seen her to the door. He had appeared astonished to find the cashier missing. The girl at the back had said that he'd gone out and wouldn't be a moment. The manager had fussed; was quite disturbed. Of course, when one came to think, a cashier was always there, otherwise how would people get their money? Probably the man had gone to lunch a little early, without saying, before the other one came back.

At the station the car was ready waiting. Bob jumped out and held the door. Miss Seeton sat in front. Behind, the Hosiggs, hand in hand, sat next to Mel, who was writing on a scribbling pad. Len Hosigg's face was sullen still; the eyes still watchful, but not wary. He leaned across and gripped Miss Seeton's arm; sat back. She managed not to wince.

"I'm so sorry," she apologized, "that the police misunderstood. Though not their fault. Or not entirely. I'm afraid the blame was largely mine. You see, I overslept. The whiskey—I'm not used to it. And then, of course, there was the tablet too." She beamed upon them. So very, very young; so shy; and so dependable. "But everything is all right now?"

"S'right," said Len.

They drove to Plummergen.

The village seethed. Somehow the word had got around. The tribal drums had beaten and the news had spread. Things had been stolen; that was undisputed. The dispute raged round who had stolen what and why? The obliging Doris Quint, in deep, shocked sympathy with the burglars' victims—"Wasn't it lucky to think them things'd all been found?"—had done her quota to incite the rumors. Miss Seeton was involved, inevitably; she'd pinched a car and ditched it; was under arrest; her license was endorsed. The Hosiggs were mixed up in it. Miss Seeton, to evade pursuit and to confuse the scent, had swum to Rye. There was dope of course. And drink, bottles of it. Whiskey had flowed in streams. Miss Seeton had held an orgy in her cottage: furniture had been smashed; cushions and curtains ripped. The Colvedens had been there; the police—you couldn't trust a soul; Miss Knight and that reporter woman; and Miss Treeves—too dreadful, you'd have thought the vicar's sister ... Shocking, the things that people did. Then, too plastered to notice it was pouring, they'd all gone on one of those midnight treasure hunts. While she, with that Hosigg, in a lorry, slipped back and pinched things. And all of this while they'd been worrying whether she'd been killed. Really. People.

Mel, unused to village gossip, enlarged, in close-up, was hopping mad. She'd give them Cow-Face Posture.

* * *

From the *Daily Negative*—March 29

THE PEACE OF THE ENGLISH COUNTRYSIDE
by Amelita Forby

*

Piece 3. *Cows in Pasture*

In peaceful Plummergen, in this small serene, sweet-tempered corner of Olde Worlde Kent, sheep graze upon the marsh, cows in the meadows. Their bleatings and their mooings echo softly through the dusk.

In peaceful Plummergen cows moo in houses too. And, apelike in their mimicry, sheep bleat in cottages.

In peaceful Plummergen, where life flows smooth and nothing ever happens; except robbery and violence—three in one night is the score to date …

Where the Brolly, working overtime on rescue work …

Where a visit to the dentist can be termed an orgy …

Where young love and nobility can be smeared and much maligned …

Where the police work night and day, to help, to guard and cherish, only to finally be misunderstood …

In peaceful Plummergen, where anything can happen—and it does—the only thing found to so far be missing is murder.

Can we now confidently wait—do you suppose—for murder too in peaceful Plummergen?

* * *

Chapter 8

Effie goffer was having the time of her life. Conducted to school, escorted from it, wherever she went one or the other of two stolid young men waited upon her. That neither of her squires liked her did not worry her. No one ever had. She was not likable. Plain and precocious, with bad manners, whenever she had goaded schoolfellows they had retaliated. Now this was changed. In the playground and on the street she could vent her spite on whom she willed in safety. One stuck-out tongue, one raised shoe, one lifted arm, and she ran to her watchdog for protection. Never before had she been important. Now she was.

Then it palled. Her favorite pastime of spying on others was impossible. When spied upon yourself you cannot spy. This irked her. Slowly it dawned that to be attended everywhere meant that your own actions were given close attention. They were playing her special game, "I Spy." On her. This was a challenge not to be ignored. She'd show them who was who. She waited for the evening changing of the guard. Then on her way home to supper and to bed she ducked from sight and vanished.

The body was found in a ditch next morning by a farm laborer on his way to work.

Plummergen was besieged. CHILD STRANGLER STRIKES AGAIN. It brought in more police. It brought the press. It brought the rubbernecks. It also brought dismay. Murder is fun to read about, but there are rules. Murder must know its place. Murder must be confined within an expected circle. But beyond all other considerations murder must—or risk its popularity—take place elsewhere. The rules were broken and the village was not pleased.

At Rytham Hall breakfast was spoiled. The papers were unread.

"I think," said Lady Colveden, "that people are chiefly shocked because they're not." Nigel looked at her. "Well, it's true," protested his mother. "You see, we should be and we aren't; or only because it's happened so near home. You know, like that woman in Shakespeare somewhere who says it shouldn't've happened in her house. Hamlet, I expect, it always is. You see, I feel I ought to care, to mind, about Effie; but I don't. She was a horrid little girl. I'm sorry for her mother—really sorry—though personally if it was me I should feel ..." She caught her husband's eye. "But that's just it, George," she justified, "that's what I'm driving at ... The whole thing's awful simply because it's not." She took another piece of toast, then drank some more tea. Looked troubled. "I'll have to go and see her mother, shan't I?" There was a silence of consent. "But what can one say? It would be even worse not to, I suppose. And you can't take anything with you which always makes things easier. At least, I can't think of anything." She addressed her son. "Can you?" He shook his head. "No, nor can I. Well, I mean you can't just walk in and say: I'm sorry your little girl's been killed and here's a pot of jam." She appealed to her husband.

"Couldn't I just leave it? Sort of—let it go?" She got no answer. "No, I thought not." She sighed, stood up, began to gather plates.

The police reaction was one of fury tinged, for the superintendent, with despair. They called in reserves, deployed in force and questioned everyone. Delphick himself examined both the Quints. The result was negative. The pathologist's report placed the time of the killing between six and eight in the evening. The rest of the forensic details, the wire, the method, the contusions, Delphick knew by heart.

Quint, at ease, was cheerful and cooperative: the sergeant in his notes described him as "cocky." Been for a walk in the afternoon, he said, just for a breather. Got home by four and had a lay-down, waiting for Doris to come back. Ticker trouble—the doc said to watch it. Delphick noted that the nervous breakdown from overwork had become heart disease, but made no comment. It wasn't altogether contradictory; the one could cause the other. The kid, Quint said, had been about the place on and off, he hadn't really noticed. After tea they'd watched the telly—muck mostly—then gone to bed. He didn't know a thing about any trouble till the milkman came.

Doris's story tallied. She'd finished off her ladies at five. That'd been at Lilikot—them they called the Nuts, and not surprising, nutty as fruitcakes both of them, only eating vegetables and such. Still crabbing about the crib. Awful that had been. Though what they'd got to crab about with everything got back she couldn't see. Anyway she was home at ten past five and got the tea. Eggs they'd had and a nice tin of spaghetti and some ham, with cheese for afters. Then, like Dick said, they'd watched the telly and gone to bed. Awful it was when they heard this morning. With all these goings-on in a piddling little place like this it made you wonder.

It made Delphick wonder. The Quints' story was straightforward enough, even likely, but there was no proof either way. Doris was very voluble. For her, forthright. It struck him she was nervous; that she was covering up. Just as, to him, the Hosiggs felt right, the Quints felt wrong. Their explanation of their presence in the village and their stories were reasonable enough and could be true; the feel was, they weren't. He'd had inquiries made and London was still checking, but so far nothing about the Quints seemed known to anyone. It was as if they'd plucked themselves out of the air and landed here. Without more to go on than feelings and vague suspicions, all confounded by that alibi, he couldn't take it further. He'd even toyed with the possibility of bringing down the landlady who had suspected her daily help of theft, on the chance that she might identify Doris. But even if he did, and if she did, he'd be no forrader. It would add no proof—merely a vague and questionable confirmation of a matter of which, he now decided, he'd already made up his mind. He looked at the younger brother. The boy was watching him. Had there been ...? Delphick was almost certain that he had caught a change of expression, a flicker too brief to analyze. Fear? The boy's face was smooth now, empty. But there had been something. The superintendent tried to make his mind a blank; to let it recapture of its own volition the impression it had received; to allow it to develop the blurred negative, snapped in the blinking of an eyelid and out of focus. Antagonism? Derision? He could not be sure. Somehow the imprint that remained, however hazy and obscure, was one of fear. And, if so, fear of what? Of him—as a stranger?—as a police officer? Of the boy's own family? How did you go about questioning a deaf-mute? Could he lip-read? Was he old enough? Exaggerating his speech, Delphick tried a question. He got his answer in strained and ugly sounds; confused babble.

Doris flared up at once. He'd leave the kid alone, she ordered. Coming here bullying kids that couldn't even speak, let alone understand. Who did he think he was? She knew her rights.

In turn Delphick studied the older couple. Dick Quint's face was unremarkable: low-browed; low cunning; thick-lipped; a little brutish; the total sum still unremarkable. In Doris there was a likeness to her brother: in her the underhung jaw and slack mouth looked unstable, weakly obstinate; the slightly protruding eyes reminded him of exophthalmic goiter. On the younger face the same features gave an appealing uncertainty of immaturity to the mouth and a rounded air of innocence to the eyes. If there was mental disorder here—and unless his instinct and conviction were at fault there must be—where did it lie?

Dick Quint's mental reaction was simple and straightforward: this busy had nothing hard on them; just doing a spot o' ferreting. Let him. He'd get sweet all of proof. Lamping the kid a bit, though, wasn't he?

Doris's response was more involved: this bit o' fuzz could stuff himself; he wasn't fly—just poking around in general, what they called routine. Let 'im. It'd get him no place. But starting on the kid was different. Doris knew her brother, knew that of the family he had the strongest will, knew that if his mind was set nothing would shift it, knew from experience that to try such a shift meant stirring dangerous depths of temper, knew too that, when he wished, he could find means to communicate with others. That Delphick should have dared to question him both scared her and enraged her. But she'd settled his hash, she decided, and given him the right-about. He'd leave the kid alone in future or she'd know why.

For Doris's brother? Who can guess what reflexes take place within a shuttered mind. Alienists may argue; psychiatrists may suggest; graphs can be drawn from stimulation of the heart or brain; but all is only guesswork. Distortion of the mind can be difficult to define and no reasoning can accurately forecast action or reaction. Cause may be argued from effect but without effect, for without an effect there is no ground for argument and in effect such argument remains but guesswork. Whether Doris's brother had understood Delphick's attempt to question him; whether in turn he had attempted to reply; whether he had understood the purpose of Delphick's visit and whether, in understanding, he had deliberately evaded could only be conjecture, conclusions drawn from imperfect information.

Delphick prepared to leave. He looked again at the brother; attractive-looking kid. He stared again at Doris and her husband, visualizing wire dangling ready from expectant hands. He felt a little sick.

At Ashford the chief inspector was regretting having freed Len Hosigg.

"If only we'd held him, Oracle, we'd know more where we stood. As it is, soon as we ride him a bit, then let him go, this happens. It looks bad."

"There'd still have been his wife," the superintendent pointed out. "And in this case my bet is on the weaker vessel."

At Delphick's request they arranged that if the Quints' van was noticed on the road it was to be stopped on a technicality and the driver's license asked for, to give them a chance to check the name and address. To insist upon seeing it in the garage the police would require a search warrant, which no responsible magistrate would grant since there was no evidence. Bob Ranger had done a scout round when the Quints weren't there; no tracks of motorcycles about the place; no traces in the shed; in fact no sign that they had ever ridden or possessed such things. Only the small van which needed cleaning and the doors of which were locked. Brinton came up with an idea. Would Delphick get Miss Seeton to go to the village school and draw all the children there?

Delphick demurred. "You're asking a lot of her. There's never been two cases in one district, Chris. And anyway I didn't know you had such faith in her."

"I haven't," retorted Brinton, "but you can't get away from it, Oracle, there was that nasty drawing of the Goffer girl and then that Lily business. All right, so it may not mean a thing, but it makes you think. We can't afford to miss a trick. The school's only small; we don't want oil paintings, just a rough idea. She'd probably run through the whole lot cheap for an all-in fee."

The superintendent rang Scotland Yard. Sir Hubert Everleigh agreed; remarking sourly that at the rate they were going it would be more economical to put Miss Seeton on the force.

The newspapers elected to harmonize on the theme of Public Indignation. The public were indignant, they declared. This was the sixth child murder, and still no arrest. It was outrageous, they asserted, that the killings should take place under the very noses of the police. Under the very nose of Superintendent Delphick of Scotland Yard, who was the officer in charge, and even staying in the actual village where the atrocity had been committed. In stressing the fact that the police were on the spot at the precise moment of the crime, the obvious implication, that they were beginning to close on their quarry, was ignored. Privately, Fleet Street's genuine indignation was reserved for the *Negative* and Mel. Mel's warning of murder in her piece, coming out the day before, must have been inspired. What was the dope? How had she got on to it? Why hadn't they all known that the Oracle was down at Plummergen? How had the *Negative* got the beat? And why hadn't the Forby used it in her stuff?

The plan which the editor of the *Daily Negative* had evolved had worked precisely as he had hoped it would. The Forby Pieces on the Battling Brolly had been dismissed by the *Negative*'s rivals as an attempt to flog a dead horse and her treatment of it had been laughed out of print as more suited to a woman's magazine than to a daily newspaper. Not for a moment had it occurred to any of them that in spite of her odd and individual treatment she was on to one of the major stories of the year where treatment mattered little while fact and an inside track were all-important.

Mel had rung her paper at intervals through the night with the news of Effie Goffer's disappearance; of the all-out police hunt; the fears for the child's safety; the use of dogs; and finally, with Delphick's consent, the belief that the child strangler was involved. This tidbit, too late for the front page, had been just in time to make the fudge. The discovery of the body, missing the Dailies, was blazoned in the Evenings. But Mel had got her beat and she was satisfied. The *Negative* too. She'd kept Miss Seeton and the Brolly out of it. To the uninitiated Miss S wasn't patently involved, and news-wise this stuff didn't fit the Pieces. She'd go on running those her own way and splash any headline stuff straight as it came in.

For the rubbernecks, the Indignant Public, their attitudes and feelings in the main were determined by their individual points of view.

"No, Gertie, not from there—the sun's full on your lens. The view from this side's better." "I really don't see the point in coming here if we don't know the exact spot." "Well, my view is it's a swizz—no point in it, no blood nor nothing."

Miss Seeton did as she was asked. She fulfilled her commission, sitting in the classrooms at the school almost opposite Dr. Knight's nursing home. She sketched some fifty little faces. The results, though they might be depressing from the artistic standpoint, were heartening for the police in a disproved fashion. However indifferently drawn, at least all the faces were complete.

Delphick was studying the sketches with care in the lounge of the George and Dragon when Mel came in for lunch. She asked if she could look them over. The superintendent was severe.

"Certainly not, Miss Forby. These are a police matter. It would be most improper. And would you mind," he added, "moving round behind me where you won't be in my light?"

Mel's face crinkled. She leaned over the back of his chair while he laid out the sketches for her benefit. There were five sheets in all; several faces to each sheet. She gave them a cursory glance, reached over his shoulder, gathered them together and slapped them face downward on his lap.

"Don't waste your time, boy, haven't you got wise to it yet? Miss S may be a good teacher, I wouldn't know, but I do know she's one hell of a bad artist. Every so often, when something strikes her and her hand takes over, then she's really got something, some quality—I don't know, it's not my field, but I do know it's there. At a guess I'd say she's inhibited."

Delphick laughed. Anyone less inhibited than Miss Seeton was difficult to imagine. "No, not inhibited; just diffident. Miss Seeton's a great believer in freedom of expression—for the really clever. Or," he grinned, "the highly trained. It's never occurred to her, and never will, that she is really clever—or could've been."

"Seems a waste. A few cartoons by her when she's in form would light things up some. Come on, boy. A drink. On me. Expense account." Mel led the way to the bar.

Delphick put the papers away and followed her. "It's not a waste, you know,' he said, "to be a contented being."

"Me, marry a crook? You must be off your head."

"Maryse ..."

"What d'you take me for?" Maryse Palstead plucked a cigarette from the pack in her handbag. "D'you think I'm going to spend the rest of my life wondering when the police are going to catch up with you? D'you think I'm going to start having heart attacks every time I meet a policeman on the street?" She stuck it between her lips. "D'you think," the cigarette waggled as she spoke, "every time I get a parking ticket, I'm going to start worrying whether it's a trick and if the next move's going to be the police coming to the house asking questions? About you?"

"Maryse ..."

"What d'you think I am?" she sneered. "Some gangster's moll?" She flicked the gold lighter he had given her and studied him over the flame. "D'you think I mean to throw away a respectable life?" She inhaled, blew smoke at him. "D'you really think," she demanded, "I'm going to live on tenterhooks for the sake of your blue eyes and curly hair?" Looking at him—the dark eyes, the straight black hair, the thin mustache—she laughed. "You must be mad, my friend. Think again."

"But, Maryse, you said ..."

"I said nothing." She was definite. She dropped the lighter onto the low table beside her, lay back, and slung her feet up on the sofa. "You have money. You want to spend it, cut a figure, play cops and robbers, disguise yourself, and build yourself up a new identity. Why not?" she mocked him. "Go ahead. That's your affair. You wanted an affair with me." Her mouth hardened. "Very well, that's mine. Where your money comes from doesn't affect me. I don't want to know about it." She flicked ash. "As far as I'm concerned you wanted to chuck your money around. Who am I to stop you? It's not my business to ask questions." He started to protest again, viciously she overspoke him. "If you want to spill your silly little soul out, telling me all you're doing, all you mean to do, all your—God save us—plans for the future, that's your lookout. But, my friend, be very sure it's not, and never will be, mine."

Dazed, the cashier dropped into the armchair facing her. His briefcase, with the money taken from the bank, lay on the floor beside an evening paper; no mention yet of him. He lifted his head to look around in wonder: at her flat; at the expensive furniture; at the ornaments; mostly bought by him; bought for the future; their future.

She watched him coldly. "You thought you'd been so clever." Her voice, reflective, almost gentle, began to sting him. "Clever?" she questioned. "The police've probably been on to you for months. Why else should they send some old harpy to the bank to start you panicking? You thought she'd given herself away. Don't make me laugh. What else d'you think she went there for? They're not fools. They wanted to get you on the run. And they have. So now you're dropping out of sight, to come popping up as someone else. You," she scoffed, "with your colored contact lenses, dyed hair, and all the rest of it. Well," with finality, "I'm dropping out too. For us, my friend, this is the end of the road."

The bank cashier was silent. The end of the road? So this was Maryse. He waited, numbed still, for the realization to penetrate. To have been so loving, so gentle, so affectionate, a gay companion, interested, encouraging him; until all his plans had included her. The jewelry he'd given her to be a safeguard, a part of their joint capital in their new life—together. All this while there was money with safety. At least, safety for her. Now that the critical moment had arrived, that the time for the change had come, time for him to throw off his old self and bury it—or rather let others bury it for him—literally: now that real danger was close, she was "dropping out." Besides, there wasn't any danger. The plan was too simple, too carefully thought out, too long worked on, for danger.

Taking money from the bank had been dead easy. All you needed was ability and nerve. He had both. But, better, he had brains. Small fiddles they were on the watch for, and would be found out quick enough. But decent amounts, once you'd been there long enough to be trusted … Forging the odd receipt of the fools who gave the bank discretionary powers on their deposit accounts. If people had so much money that they could leave it lying about idle and giving the bank charge of it while they went gallivanting abroad, sometimes for years on end, they were asking for it to be lifted by someone with sense and a little courage. It wouldn't even hurt them. The bank would have to make it up. Well, he'd had a good run for their money and had got it past the accountants three years running. He'd no complaints. A house bought and paid for, Maryse's jewelry, the furniture and the Rover, and more than thirty-five thousand in cash and securities, which with his knowledge he should be able to double within a couple of years. And once you'd got proper capital, money made itself.

The "simple plan" was simply: to build a new identity in Brettenden as a man of some substance; to kill his old identity by having his charred remains found in the burned-out wreck of his old car; then, with the absconding bank cashier's body identified and the hunt over, to settle down in Brettenden with a new name, his house, a car, and finally Maryse.

His one outstanding feature was the curious light blue of his eyes. Three years before, during his holiday, he had flown to Munich to be fitted with colored microlenses. By wearing them for lengthening periods at night he had become so accustomed to them that he could wear them indefinitely without discomfort. The deep brown, almost black, eyes changed the whole effect of his personality. His fair wavy hair darkened and straightened with a washable dye and wearing a pencil-thin mustache, he was unrecognizable. This he had proved, after a year's practice, by going to the bank where he was employed, during his next yearly holiday, and opening an account there under his chosen alias. If any suspicion had been aroused it was to have been a semi-serious joke: a man keen on his work, testing security and possibilities of fraud; trying to anticipate experience. The experiment worked and the account was accepted without question. With growing confidence in his new guise he bought a house on the outskirts of Brettenden, a Rover automatic, passed tests and acquired a driving license for this second self. To neighbors he gave out that business would keep him on the move for a short time yet, after which he hoped to settle down. It seemed natural therefore that the rather foreign-looking gentleman who had taken Ivy Manse was only glimpsed briefly at infrequent weekends. It was unlikely in the extreme that this gentleman of means would ever be connected with the bank cashier of none who drove from his Ashford lodgings to his work at Brettenden in a dilapidated fourth-hand car.

Maryse Palstead was the only deviation from his original design. Casually met at a party, he was attracted; she was not. Determined to make an impression, he took her out, spent money on her, a treatment to which she responded. He became infatuated; so, it appeared, did she. He began to drop hints until finally he told her of all he was doing; all he meant to do. She had been helpful with ideas: to invest in jewelry; to open a deposit account in his new character and to milk it in his old. This last delighted him: a perfect method of robbing Peter to pay Paul with the bank as the patsy who, in repaying Peter, would also unwittingly repay Paul. Unwilling to commit herself before their scheme had proved itself safe and successful, Maryse settled that they should not marry until at least three months after his supposed death.

The bank cashier shifted in his chair; his face had grown very pale. So this was the end. Of the road. Of Maryse. How right she was. He must have been mad: telling her all his plans; spilling his silly little soul. She could spill on him. His eyes were fixed unseeing on the newspaper by his feet. The words began to focus. CHILD STRANGLER STRIKES AGAIN, ARE PLUMMERGEN BURGLARIES CONNECTED? Connected? Connected. His mind started to work. It all dropped into place. He noted the time on his wristwatch: twenty past ten. Yes—it all dropped into place; it fitted. But he mustn't waste time.

He got up. "I'll get a drink."

"I don't want one."

"I do."

He went to the kitchenette, clinked some glasses, opened a drawer. A few odd tools, a screwdriver, pliers and—he'd been right—a coil of picture wire. He cut a length. He clinked a glass again, returned to the sitting room.

Maryse heard him behind her. "Finish it. And then get out. For good." She leaned across the table and ground her cigarette out in an ashtray.

"I will." From behind the sofa he bent forward and, wrists crossed, dropped the loop of wire over her head as she sat back. He pulled. She reared up open-mouthed and clutching. He pulled until the wire furrowed his hands: let go. The body slumped in an untidy heap.

Precise, an automaton, he took her handbag, hefted the gold lighter, pocketed it, took the notes and loose change, tossed the bag aside, went to the bedroom, found her jewel case, smashed it and threw the jewels, uninsured, unlisted, into his briefcase. He flung open drawers and cupboards, strewed the contents. He picked up his newspaper and coat and left the flat.

The police would be on the watch by now for his old car. Well, they weren't likely to find it till he meant them to. He'd have to use it tonight, but once he'd collected it he shouldn't be on a main road for long. It was a slight risk, but one he'd got to take. The only bad moment had been slipping into the Brettenden house unnoticed to change and take the Rover. That had come off: he'd not been seen.

He took the direct route from Ashford to the highway. About two miles short of it he turned off onto a secondary road, off that again into a narrow lane leading past a disused quarry. At the top of the quarry face, to his right, a short grass slope led straight to the edge. To his left there were bushes and scrub backed by a spinney. He maneuvered the car in behind the bushes, careful not to scratch it on the loosely clustered brambles. His old car was there waiting for him, its number plates well muddied. He inspected them with the aid of a flashlight and decided that they were illegible from any distance without being too noticeably obscured. He got in, removed his wristwatch, inscribed with his initials, and laid it on the passenger seat, took a notecase containing his old driving license and insurance certificate and pushed them down into the upholstery behind him. Keeping to side roads, he drove north, cut across to the A.20 and went slowly back toward Maidstone. He'd meant to allow two or three nights for this operation to give himself plenty of choice to pick from, but now that wretched old woman at the bank'd got him on the run he'd have to take potluck and hope for the best.

A hitchhiker thumbed a lift. He slowed the car to a crawl: a kid with a large knapsack strapped to his back. He accelerated. A few minutes later another thumb was raised. One thing you could rely on; hitchhikers were always plentiful. Again he slowed. This one looked better. He stopped the car, leaned across, and opened the door.

"Dover?" the hiker asked. He bent down, his face showing in the interior light. Thirtyish, carrying a parcel. He'd do.

"Right," said the bank cashier, "if you don't mind if we go round a bit. I've got something to do on the way. Won't take a moment or two. Oh, hang on—" as the other was getting in. He picked up his watch from the passenger seat. "Mind holding onto this? Safer still, put it on if you would. Got a burn on my wrist and it rubs it. I don't want it falling down between the seats."

The hiker was surprised, shrugged. "Okay." He strapped on the watch.

Bypassing Maidstone, the bank cashier continued down the highway, then forked left. Two miles later he branched right onto the secondary road, from that turned into the narrow lane. He offered his passenger a cigarette, took one himself, and lit them. The car climbed steeply. He swung it left toward the bushes and scrub, spun the wheel and brought the car round in a half circle, switching off the headlights. He stopped, leaving the gears in neutral, the brake off, and the engine running.

"Hang on. Won't be a minute." Dropping his lighted cigarette on the floor, he jumped out and ran to the back of the car.

The hiker turned. "Hey, oughtn't you to …" He felt the movement, panicked for the door handle. "You fool, you didn't …"

The rest was lost as the car left the grass to turn a tired somersault in the air.

Time was suspended, stretched and endless. Then below: a mineral explosion; an animal scream; the tintamar of metal; tinkling glass. Silence. Faintly, a mewing. A whimper wetly choked. Silence.

The bank cashier looked down; watching, waiting. It must work; it had to. Whenever you read of a car crashing from a height the big danger was fire. And with the engine running and a spare can of petrol with a loosened cap in the back, and two lighted cigarettes, it couldn't fail. There was no sign of light: the sidelamps must have been smashed in the fall. His imagination had held him rooted there an hour when after a few seconds the darkness beneath him was flawed by a tiny flicker of red. It died. His heartbeat lurched. The flicker came again: erupted suddenly, an orange flower red-centered. The sound of the explosion came to him as the redness streaked in flames.

Chapter 9

The fire at the quarry had been seen from a farm. By the time the fire brigade had arrived and the police had been sent for, there was little to do except to wait for the debris to cool sufficiently to permit an examination. A young constable helped the ambulance men to extricate the body but when it fell apart so did he and the inspector assigned to the case sent him back to the hospital to be treated for shock. A man was left in charge and arrangements were made for the remains of the car to be trucked into Asford, where the scientific squad could examine them in the morning. The front number plate was still readable and the hospital sent over an initialed wristwatch found with the corpse; so that by the time Chief Inspector Brinton arrived after a hearty breakfast the unpleasing details and a tentative identification were waiting for him on his desk. The identification was confirmed within an hour when the scientific department produced the scorched portion of a driver's license and a burned scrap of paper on which they had managed to bring up some figures they claimed were part of an insurance certificate. The corpse was officially recognized as that of the missing bank cashier; the explanation of his death being accredited to suicide—or plain idiocy. The case was closed. It opened again before lunch.

Maryse Palstead's murder was discovered by her daily help when she arrived at ten o'clock. She screamed, she called for help, she called the tenants of the neighboring flats who in their turn called neighbors and, after all had had just one quick look, the daily called the porter who called the landlord who finally called the police.

The inspector who was sent to deal with the case, having scrutinized the wire and the method, rang headquarters. Chief Inspector Brinton then rang Delphick to tell him that another of his little specialties had cropped up, remarking that if the Oracle's presence meant that wire neckties were going to be all the rage in Kent, all right, he himself was resigning as from last Monday week.

When Delphick arrived in Ashford the local inspector handed the case over to him with relief. Delphick, after a brief inspection, handed it back. Not the child strangler, he judged. An imitation; and a poor imitation at that. They would wait for the pathologist's report, but he was fairly certain that more force and different wire had been used. He picked up the length lying near the body. The marks of the twisted strands from the picture wire were scored deeply into the neck, cutting the skin in two places. Also the bruising was more extensive. Delphick, however, agreed to assist with the questioning. From the daily help, who was by now well into her third pot of tea, they learned: that her eldest was doing nicely—worked in a garage; her second were a layabout—didn't seem to settle; that her daughter weren't above a bit—whatever that might mean; her youngest was still at school; and her husband didn't above half—which clarified nothing except that his daughter appeared to be taking after him. She herself were all of a thing which was really no more than you might expect seeing she hadn't expected, and if she had, and if only somebody'd told her, she wouldn't've stayed—not a day. Come to think of it she could say, and she'd say it straight, she'd never in her life been more surprised. The Ashford inspector fumed. Delphick, by patience, elicited the information that Miss Palstead were a bit of a flighty one, which appeared to be the sum total of the lady's knowledge of her late employer.

The porter was more helpful. Yes, Miss Palstead had had a lot of boy friends, but only one regular, specially just recent. The description of the regular and of his car tallied with a "Wanted for Questioning" notice for a cashier, posted the day before, on information supplied by a bank in Brettenden. The inspector debated. A keen constable produced his notebook in which he had made a copy of the notice. The inspector again telephoned the station. Headquarters got things moving and the suspicion was confirmed when they compared fingerprints taken from her flat and his lodgings. By teatime the cashier's case was again closed, with the Palstead case neatly tucked inside it, and all was once more serene.

Plummergen was relieved: the storm clouds that had gathered had now passed. Too dreadful of course as Effie's murder had been and, more dreadful because more material, the burglaries, obviously the village's involvement, had been pure chance. Lightning, as anyone knew, never struck in the same place; which was a comfort.

It comforted the vicar's sister. "It's a comfort," said Miss Treeves, "to know that everything is settled and that it was no one in the village after all. I suppose one shouldn't think that way but I'm bound to say, Arthur," Molly Treeves handed her brother his second cup of coffee, "it's a relief that that awful man at the bank is dead. I must admit I never really liked him. He always had such a bored manner; as if he couldn't be bothered. Didn't you notice it?"

The vicar put in two lumps and stirred. "Notice?" he asked.

"Yes." She rose and began to collect the lunch plates. "When you think that all the time with that Ashford woman ... Naturally I'm sorry for her but I can't help feeling in a way she got what she deserved. And then holding up the post office here and killing Effie—it must, have been insanity." She dumped the stacked plates on a tray, the cutlery on top. "And stealing from houses too—once you've started I suppose you can't stop." She took the coffee pot. "I know we shouldn't say so," she put the pot and her cup on the tray, "but quite honestly I think death is the best answer, don't you?" She picked up the tray. "Well, don't you?" she repeated from the doorway when her brother remained silent. She went out.

Did he? Reverend Arthur wondered. The question, like so many of the riddles concerning Human Misbehavior and the Divine Aftermath, was complicated. And that it should have proved to be a woman—it made it infinitely worse. He had quite thought the police had spoken of a man. For the hundredth time he vowed that he would take more notice, pay more attention. Sternly he tried to conjure up a vision of the woman cashier with a bored manner. She refused to materialize. He sighed; acknowledged humbly, if it weren't for Molly, he wouldn't always know quite where he stood. What was it she had asked him? "Didn't he?" "Oh, yes," he told an empty room, "I do."

The ladies of Lilikot could not of course be comforted for the too outrageous insinuations by the police regarding the value of their stolen treasures—though as everyone knew it was only too easy for certain people to hold on to the genuine articles, have them copied, and then return the imitation—but it was a relief to know that the murders had been done by someone outside the village. The robberies of course were a different matter. You tried to be fair and make allowances, but it was only too obvious, without mentioning names, that there was a lot more there than met the eye. As for that unspeakable reporter with her *cows* … That person had been told a piece of your mind that made it all too clear what you thought of her. That their own bank should have had the bad taste to become involved in the scandal through its cashier they looked upon as an affront. Miss Nuttel came up with the solution.

"I shall transfer my account."

At Rytham Hall comfort was in question.

"It's nice to know that it's all finished." Lady Colveden handed coffee to Nigel, who passed it to his father. "Even if you don't believe it."

"And you don't?" asked her son.

"Well, no, I don't. Of course naturally I can see it from the police point of view; it saves them a lot of trouble. But having love affairs in Ashford and fiddling with funds at the bank are quite a different matter to chasing round the countryside and killing children." Both her husband and her son's expression queried her statement. She considered. "It seems perfectly clear to me. If you're having an affair in Ashford—though frankly it's not the place I should choose—and you're getting tired of it or the other person's being tiresome and there's a bit of wire lying handy, I can quite imagine strangling them on the spur of the moment. And as for fiddling cash—well, anybody would if they knew how. But all that's quite a different story to post offices and Effie." She gave herself a nod of encouragement. "You'll find I'm right. All the newspapers have gone home, but you notice Miss Forby hasn't, and nor have the superintendent and his sergeant. If," she concluded in triumph, "it was all finished they would have."

At the Dunnihoe cottage youth was too young to question comfort.

"Oh, Len, it's wunners, isn't it?" Lil Hosigg cut a large portion of suet pudding, poured golden syrup over it, and handed it to him. "I mean with us in the clear with the police and everything. 'Course it's not going to be nice with the case being done again and everything about that man mum married and what he did coming out, or tried on anyway. You should never've kept quiet, I wanted to speak up, you know I did, and I could've made Rosie too, but it'll blow over and I think it's wunners." She looked at him for a few seconds yearningly. "You're wunners too, you know. And it's all really because of that funny little old geyser who smiled at us when we first come here, and when that kid tried to jump in front of the car said how clever you was to stop, 'stead of creating as most would. And then when you looked after her like you did, 'stead of just saying thanks and forgetting it, went charging off to the police to tell them what she thought of you and got everything put right and did that lovely picture of you which she gave me' cause I asked her if she'd sell it." She glowed at him. "And it's no good you looking po-faced, it's a real picture by an artist just like you are and I wouldn't be without it not for anything. I'm going to put glass over it and hang it up. I like her she's nice. And now the police know what you're like and that London chap's going to see the appro business's put right, and it wasn't nobody here after all but somebody over to Ashford, it's all finished and it's all wunners." She smiled with pride. "Isn't it, you great gorm?"

The sullen face transformed. Wonder and love welled up to overspill in speech. "S'right," said Len.

* * *

No comfort at Saturday Stop.

"Sweet bloshing nothing, zero, nothing, that's all we got on this flub. You, you knows it all, don't you? The Smoke getting too hot for us you said. Have another bash in Kent, some little place where they won't know from their bottoms up, you said. Dead easy like falling off a log, and we clean up a bomb and back to the Smoke you said. Looks like it, don't it?" Dick Quint was savage. " 'Stead of which we're stuck in this drum, spent all our gelt and near enough got tumbled by the busies."

"Getting milky?" scoffed Doris. "Who does it all round here? Me. Slog my guts out all day casing the joints, seeing which houses're worth a lift and setting it up. And then cooking for you two, you and the kid, and what d'you do? Sit around on your fannies doing sweet all."

"And that's a lot of madam," he flung at her. "Who does the job when it comes to it? And when I done it what's the touch, half the stuff was fake. Your trouble's you can't tell slap-up stuff from snide. Them two old tarts at the Nut House, they spruced you proper."

Doris was indignant. "How was I to know? 'It's all too, too valuable,' " she mimicked. "People's got no right to lie about their stuff, putting it on. Downright dishonest, don't know where you are. But the haul from the other two was good enough."

"And what good did that do to us?" he sneered. "Lost the lot didn't we when that old trot slung her mush through the windshield and pitched us in the ditch."

"That one, that's twice she done us, and that brolly of hers, she's put a hoodoo on us."

Dick Quint shrugged. "Hoodoo, voodoo, what's the diff? All we got for it's fuzz all over the shop like fleas, with that Oracle round just after we got back'n catching you with your hair all wet."

"Well, what odds?" Doris defended herself. "I chatted him up all right. I don't go for busies with posh talk, he's a right piece of toffee that one."

"You chatted him," he gibed. "He's maybe a toff but he's leary. Came again didn't he? With his gorilla mucking about the garden and poking into the shed."

"Well, he couldn't find nothing, no tracks nor nothing, and the bikes were safe enough, the van were locked, and sergeant or no he couldn't go poking into that, it's against the law."

"And did you latch on to how the Oracle was eyeing the nutcase kid?" Quint glared at his brother-in-law.

"Leave the kid alone," flashed Doris.

"Leave him?" he retorted. "Too right I'll leave him. A mugger for crissakes. You're a nutter yourself to let him—a right family of nuts. What's he want to put the mug on kids for? Whyn't you stop it?"

"Stop him yourself why don't you?" She gave her brother a sideways glance. "You know how he gets his rag out if you spur him." Her hand went protectively to her neck. "Once was enough for me. If you'd not been so quick to clout him I'd've had it. I'm not risking that again thank you. He's all right if you let him be—'sides," she tossed her head, "it don't do no harm s'long as he's careful. Nobody's suspected him have they? Nor likely to. And he don't get much fun the way he is. What's a few kids?"

"He'll end by pushing us all through the big gates. Why don't he grow up? Seventeen—and look at him, a Peter Pansy for crissakes. If he must be a croaker why can't he croak somebody useful—crease that old trot with the mush, she's earned her lot? What's the fuzz coming to using old tarts like that?" The deaf-and-dumb youth watched their lips, straining to follow. He nodded to himself and smiled. His hand went to his pocket. "A break for us," went on Dick Quint, "the busies've settled for that money pusher at the bank, puts us in the clear, but we're flat and we got to get gelt—and I got that fixed. I've been touting around with the Ashford wise boys—call themselves the Choppers—'n it's all set up. Saturday they've a hop on here at the village hall'n the Choppers're coming over to break it up."

"Where's that get us?"

"Gives us cover. While they're stirring it up we'll bash a drum or two. Them Colvedens for a start, she sports a blosh-ing great diamond on her mitt—I seen it. There must be a mint of stuff knocking around the Hall."

"That lot won't be at the hop," Doris pointed out, "you won't catch the likes of them hoofing it with a lot of swedes."

"We play it like the P.O. jobs," he answered. "Rush 'em, stick'em up, lock 'em in somewhere, and if they shout crease 'em. I got a heater in Ashford—what a dump, think

I were asking for gold not a gun—and this'll be one time," he added venomously, "the old trot won't get no chance to stick her brolly in our backsides'n swipe the heater and the take."

The deaf youngster sat relaxed, dreaming, a happy indulgence on the too-young face. A length of wire with a wooden grip at each end swung idly in his hand.

For Mel Forby there was comfort in the post. Returning to the pub she brooded over a suggestion from the *Negative:* to rename the village and to run her Pieces as a strip cartoon. A strip …? Maybe a broadcast diary …? Maybe America …? Looked like she'd got it made. A little old lady stopped her in the Street. Uh huh, thought Mel, more trouble coming up from "Cows in P."

"So mischievous," hissed her interceptor, "your Pieces in the paper. Such humor. It takes a stranger to see us as we are." She wagged a forefinger. "So clever, you Americans."

"Us which?" demanded a dumbfounded Mel.

"Yes," said Miss Wicks. "And so discerning. A niece of mine is living in the States. You've probably seen her there, her name is Sybil."

Mel patted the frail shoulder. "Nay, lass, th'art goomed. Oiye coom fra Liverpule. And that I guess's the nearest to the States I've been."

The small face puckered, the withered mouth opened—Save us, thought Mel, she's going to cry—till "Tee-hee!" came from it. The old lady tapped her playfully on the arm, her dentures gleamed before she turned. Mel turned in turn to watch entranced as Miss Wicks crossed the Street and tee-heed her way home.

Well, there was a natural for a strip. A strip cartoon ... Reward for virtue? Trying to give a hand to our Miss S? Meanwhile, from the news angle she was staying put. It was over? Yeah? The Oracle hadn't shifted—or Bob Ranger. Till they went, she stayed.

So, in the comfort of normality, with danger and death receding to a town, the village was itself again, could breathe again, could now discuss the "truth" again about its neighbors without the uncomfortable feeling that the "truth" in the discussion might be the truth in fact.

In police work storm clouds rarely pass, they move, and the police move with them, to gather somewhere else; since threats to people and property are perennial. However, the Ashford Division took comfort from the fact that they had shown the Yard how to handle a case which had disturbed the whole country. That Brinton's premise that the Choppers were involved was wrong and that, in the event, the local force had had little to do beyond mopping-up operations did not signify; what counted was the truth that emerged from the mopping. It was on this question of truth that the police were divided.

The Ashford Division might be satisfied, but Delphick expressed doubts. Miss Palstead was known to have had jewelry. Where was it? The bank cashier had stolen and embezzled a lot of money. Where was it?

"Blued," suggested Chief Inspector Brinton. "Why look for trouble when there isn't any? Especially as for once we're not up to our necks in hitches and high jinks thanks to your Miss Seeton keeping her brolly out of it."

Since it wasn't his case, Delphick refrained from pressing the matter in view of his friend's evident pleasure that chummies were once more behaving normally as chummies should, tidying up their dirty little messes as they went along and generally giving the police as little trouble as possible. However, with the prevailing feeling in the division that the child strangling case was over and the killer accounted for, Delphick refused to agree. Brinton himself was prepared to allow that the Oracle could be right on this since the pathologist's report on the Palstead woman tended to confirm the superintendent's suspicions. Different wire and more force had been used than in any of the child garrotings to date. Previously there had been no lacerations and in the woman's case the pressure on the sterno-cleido-they-did-dream-'em-up-mastoid muscles had been more severe, causing deeper contusions. The watch on the Quints and the lookout for their van, therefore, would be kept, but Delphick was afraid that this watch would tend to be perfunctory. Privately he was convinced that Effie Goffer's murder had been the result of a relaxation of care on the part of her guards when the detention of young Hosigg had momentarily been considered to be the end of the case. He had therefore decided that he and the sergeant would, so far as was possible, keep a vigil of their own.

He was surprised that the Quints had stayed. By now he had become convinced in his own mind of their guilt in spite of their alibi for the post-office affair and the lack of any concrete evidence against them. In view of this, after the fiasco of their recent attempts at burglary owing to Miss Seeton's interference and the consequent presence of the police in the village, he would have expected them to get out and try elsewhere. Perhaps they were planning a last effort to recoup their losses and pay their expenses. But at least he felt there should be no further threat to life at the moment. Had there been he was certain it would have shown in Miss Seeton's sketches at the school. Those had covered all the children. All ...? No, not all, Delphick suddenly realized. The deaf-and-dumb child, through not attending school, had been missed out. It seemed unlikely that there was any danger there. If either of the Quints had wished to get rid of him they'd had plenty of opportunity in the past. And Doris in any case seemed ready enough to leap to her brother's defense. Still—best be safe. After all. Miss Seeton had seen the boy and a rough sketch from memory would tell him all he needed. He'd go over to Sweetbriars at once, he decided. It was a godsend Miss Seeton rarely made difficulties when asked for a drawing. As a professional artist all her life to be asked for a drawing was a normal request.

Miss Seeton was in her garden. At last she had found time to get down to the grass in the beds. Such a relief that everything was settled now. Though naturally very tragic. She dug her fork into the earth. Oh dear—there were so many different kinds. One had always thought of grass as grass. But, no. There was this ordinary kind; she shook it to free the earth, which scattered over her skirt. And then there was that business at the bank. And this tufted kind. So very difficult, she tugged, to get out. Really very improper. Somehow, with people in a position of trust, like a cashier ... And this dreadful thing that people called couch, though Mr. Green-finger called it something quite different, which you couldn't get out at all. Now, where was she? Ah, yes. Trust. It seemed so much worse. Quite shocking. There was a rumble as Stan Bloomer passed her with the garden roller. So very heavy. He'd stationed it near the French window for a day or two while the ground was right for rolling, and at first she'd been quite nervous lest it might roll down the slope of the lawn on top of her while she was weeding. But he'd put a triangular piece of wood—what had he called it? Of course; a chuck. Or was it chock? It was so difficult, sometimes, to understand quite what Stan was saying. When he spoke at all, that was. Mostly he just beamed at one and said, "Ah." Unless, of course, one knew exactly what he intended to say. And it did. Stop it rolling down, she meant.

A shadow fell across the bed. Miss Seeton looked up, then smiled.

"Oh, Superintendent, I'm sorry. I didn't hear you. And with the roller, I thought it was Stan." She began to rise.

Delphick stayed her. "No, at least let me help. You haven't much more to do." He squatted on his heels, took a trowel and together they finished weeding the bed in a companionable silence.

The weeds disposed of and the tools cleaned and oiled, they retired to the sitting room, where the superintendent asked her if she would mind attempting a memory sketch of the deaf-and-dumb child.

Miss Seeton was penitent. "I'm so sorry. How very remiss of me. I knew, of course, that you wanted pictures of all the children here when I went to the school. I should have remembered him. Particularly as I do feel that he should have been sent to a proper school for that kind of thing." She went to her writing desk and began to sort out paper and pencils.

"A slight impression is all I need," Delphick assured her.

Miss Seeton remained for a few moments, pencil poised, thoughtful, surprised. "You know, I realize it was very careless on my part, but it's only just occurred to me: somehow I've never thought of him as a child." She set to work.

Delphick waited. Suddenly Miss Seeton dropped her pencil and stood up. "Please." She moved away, her hands agitated. "I'm not happy about this. I don't want to go on with it, I mean. I can't, that is." She turned to Delphick in appeal. "I'm not happy about it," she repeated a little desperately. "Please."

Chapter 10

Delphick paced the living room in the family's half of the nursing home. Mrs. Knight had apologized that her husband was delayed but something had cropped up: one of the doctors from the Brettenden clinic had brought a case over for consultation which was unusual on a Saturday morning. But Dr. Knight shouldn't be very long. She had offered coffee. Delphick had thanked her but refused and after a look at his face she had thought it better to leave him to his own devices.

The superintendent stopped at the table on which he had placed a folder containing three of Miss Seeton's sketches. He laid them out and remained there pondering on the most recent of them. Wondering. Puzzling. This was one of those vital line drawings that Mel Forby called "really something." Or rather the completed half was vital. No—that was wrong, he recognized. There was vitality, there was threat, something repulsive in the blank, untouched whiteness where the other half of the face should be. Down the page ran a straight thick line. On one side there glowed the rather pretty, boyish face—but somehow not attractive, not young. The other half … Not the blurred death mask he might have expected.

Here there was no other half. It was as if someone had drawn a line through a completed portrait—a portrait so vivid as to be almost a living face—slashed one half of that face away and stuck it on a plain sheet of paper.

The result was curious. Monstrous and pathetic in one. He remembered Miss Seeton's distress over the drawing; her abrupt refusal to finish it. Although she hadn't realized it, it was, he thought, finished. Everything he needed to know was here in front of him he was sure, if only he could read it. A flicker in his mind: there was something else. What was it? Delphick searched his memory. He studied the two other sketches: that of the dead boy at Lewisham and the one of Effie Goffer. Of course—that was it. The other side. In both the previous ones it was the right side that was blurred. In this the left was blank. Right? Left? Delphick struggled with it; tried to place himself in the drawings. The right side then became one's left, which by convention stood for heart—for living. The left, the subject's right … He cast his mind back to the course he had taken in forensic medicine. Yes, the right side held, if he remembered, one of the carotid arteries. This supplied the brain. Could it then stand for brain? In the portraits of the two dead children the living side was shrouded. Here, though life was clear, the brain was missing. Allusion? Illusion? Delphick tried to be dispassionate, to rid himself of the hypnotic power the drawing held; to analyze. Was he being too fanciful? Or was there after all significance in this?

The door opened and Dr. Knight hurried in. "Sorry to've kept you. Fool of a woman's got wind and thinks she's pregnant. Why call me in? I'm not a gynecologist. Fontiss was certain of his diagnosis but thought it might be due to nervous causes. She's got a cause to be nervous. Husband's in the army, been abroad a year. Her trouble's conscience mixed with indigestion. I can't help her. Fontiss had already told her she needs a tablet not a midwife. Good man, Fontiss—sound. Now what's your trouble?" He joined Delphick at the table; noted the drawings. "The little Seeton been up to her tricks again? Or d'you need another lecture on our old friend, the split mind?"

"I have an idea it's the latter," replied Delphick. He indicated the table. "Though Miss Seeton as you can see—and guessed—comes into it. She 's sent me another riddle; and this one I can't solve."

"You think I can?" The doctor's eyebrows quirked. "Well, I prescribed another dose of murder for her and from what I've heard she's been taking it by the pint." He looked down. "What've you got here? And what's your problem?" He was silent for a space. "Don't like 'em y'know. Very unpleasant. Her work, I suppose? This," he pointed to the Effie Goffer portrait, "must be the one she came to me about. Never saw it, but Anne told me. The Seeton said she'd been trying to draw the Goffer brat, but couldn't. Thought she'd had a stroke. Rubbish. Never met anyone fitter. Beats me how she does it at her age."

Delphick gave a fleeting grin. "Yoga exercises."

Dr. Knight looked up. "Oh, that's her secret, is it? No wonder then. Sensible little woman." He bent over the table again. "Now this one," he pointed to the last of the sketches, "this I consider most unpleasant." He continued to study it. "Most unpleasant," he repeated. "What's she drawn the line for?" he asked suddenly. "Why didn't she finish it?"

Delphick moved to an armchair and sat down. "She was upset—and said she wouldn't. Or couldn't." He frowned.

"I have a feeling she did—without knowing it. I think it's complete as it stands."

"Do you?" Dr. Knight hooked a chair forward with his foot and sat. He looked at Delphick over the table. "Then I should say your mind could bear investigation. You trying to indulge in some extrasensory piffle? Or suggesting she does?"

"Is that so impossible?"

Dr. Knight glowered. "Hogwash. But then I'm only a poor nerve specialist. Who is this anyway?"

Delphick described Miss Seeton's drawings of the school children; told the doctor something of his suspicions and his reasons for them. And finally his request for the last sketch when he realized that this one child had been missed.

"Child?" rapped the doctor. "That's not a child." He tapped the sketch. "This is a case of dwarfism, Lorain-Levy type, I should say." Marking the superintendent's blank expression, he added impatiently, "Someone of childish stature and proportions. That's if this picture's accurate or has any meaning at all. Late teens, from the look of him."

Delphick puzzled. "I'd noticed the half that was there was a good likeness but that she'd missed the childish quality."

"No, not missed," declared the doctor. "If this is correct it's not there. Should say you'd let yourself be fooled by the young man's coloring and expression. Artists if they know their job go deeper than that. You'd get the same thing in a good black-and-white photograph. Look, man," his finger traced the points, "look at that eye; the setting's starting to hollow; the mouth—you don't get that firmness in a child's; or the beginning of a groove at the corner of the lip. Look at the jaw: have you ever seen that hardening of the line, that jut at the angle, in a child? But," his finger went lower, "the neck's your proof. A child's neck can be thin or fat, but it's unformed. And this—" the finger tracked a line, "if the other half of that was there you'd have an Adam's apple."

Once it had been pointed out Delphick could see it: the older face lurking beneath the childish front. And once seen he could see it no other way. Suddenly he remembered Miss Seeton's "You know, Superintendent … I've never thought of him as a child." He began to calculate. "Tell me, doctor, if that's the boy's age group, with such a handicap—and being deaf and consequently dumb, from birth—could puberty come into it? Might adolescence affect such a boy badly, make him break out like this? What I'm getting at is, could killing children be a form of compensation? Killing people his own size in order to prove himself. Does that make sense?"

"Puberty? No." Dr. Knight dismissed it. "With the Lorain-Levys, you'll get a state of sexual infantilism. But the intelligence would be perfectly normal. Mind you, I'm no authority. I'm not an alienist nor a specialist on human physiology, but certainly reduced activity of the eosinophile cells wouldn't in itself affect the brain. And the deafness has nothing to do with it—pure accident of birth. What's his speech like? Know where he was trained?"

Delphick thought. "So far as I know he can't talk at all. I imagine he's never had any training. I should say his sister's always kept him with her."

"Oh." Dr. Knight weighed the information. "Then that's a different story. Your idea—though medical poppycock—might make horse sense. Trouble with deformities is learning to live with 'em. If your young man is being tied to his sister's apron strings—she's married, isn't she, and he lives with 'em?—then he could be getting a bit above himself now he's growing up. Fatal, making people dependent on you. Take mothers with only sons: keep them dependent and they'll kick you in the teeth, or somewhere else, eventually. This sister business sounds the same. If she's kept him as a puppet all his life he might well be feeling his oats by now. Decide to strike out on his own and show them a thing or two. What you're suggesting's a paranoia induced by an original handicap, in this case deafness, aggravated by the conditions of a moronic upbringing until it's become a psychosis. H'm. Difficult to blame him. The fault of course would lie with the girl. Sorry I'm not more helpful," he pushed two of the drawings back into the folder and stood up with the last of them in his hand, "but with these sort of questions there's no yes or no. However," he faced Delphick, "if you want my opinion—off the record and without prejudice—from what you've told me I should say, yes, you're probably right." He gave the sketch a last glance before slipping it in with the others. "Most unpleasant." He handed the folder to Delphick. The telephone buzzed. The doctor picked up the extension, listened, then passed over the receiver. "Young Bob. For you."

Delphick listened to his sergeant's report without comment; said, "Right." and put the receiver back. He looked dazed.

"More trouble?" asked the doctor.

The superintendent put his hand to his forehead and smacked it. It didn't really help but it expressed his feelings. "Bob'll be here in a few minutes with the car. Ashford've just come through with some story: they say Miss Seeton's revived a corpse and gone driving with it."

"Never a dull moment," remarked Dr. Knight. "Who's the corpse?"

"A bank cashier who absconded with funds, killed his mistress in Ashford, and some charred remains found in his burned-out car were identified as his the other day. It struck me as fishy at the time—too opportune, with all the cash and her jewelry still on the missing list. But how the devil," Delphick went into the hall, "has Miss Seeton got in on it? There's no connection." He paused in buttoning his coat. "I suppose she might have seen him. He worked in Brettenden. But how's she met up with him now? If he's alive, surely he wouldn't be hanging around in Brettenden of all places. Anyway they've given us an address to start on."

The doctor followed him to the doors. "Worried about her, aren't you?"

Delphick turned on him almost savagely. "Well, wouldn't you be? If it is him, he's killed twice already. If she can identify him that's the end of her."

Dr. Knight held one of the swing doors open. "See your point, but don't give up. She's indestructible, that one. She'll probably greet you with 'Good gracious. Superintendent, how fortunate.' "

Delphick relaxed and laughed. He went out and down the steps as Bob arrived.

The check for the sketches at the school reached her addressed as before to "MissEss." So very generous of the police. And, of course, most helpful. One would not like to feel that the superintendent was doing it out of kindness. However, when one considered, he did always seem quite insistent, even firm, about what he wanted. Though with regard to that last one … She was very sorry not to have been of use. And more sorry to have behaved rather stupidly.

Really, at one's age, to allow oneself to become emotional. Miss Seeton pursed her lips in distaste. Well, it was best forgotten. She must remember to go to the bank. In some ways, now, one was bound to acknowledge that it was pleasanter. Though still, of course, quite deplorable. But, then again, one must admit that the poor man had paid for his folly. Such a dreadful way to die. But there was no denying that it was pleasanter. To go to the bank, that was. Though when one thought of that woman that he'd kept in Ashford and then killed … Much better not to think of it. She had some shopping to do in Brettenden and she could deposit the check at the same time and save postage. Because that nice Mr. Jestin—such a good idea, having those plaques on the counter telling one the cashier's name—though still very young, surely, to have been promoted to chief cashier, was, one felt, quite reliable. And also very pleasant. And greeted one by name with "Good morning" or "Good afternoon" as the case might be. And certainly never made one feel that one was wasting his time.

At the bank Miss Seeton dumped her shopping on the counter and began to fill in a slip. So fortunate that there were only three people before her. Sometimes one had to wait quite a while. The man at the head of the queue spoke to the cashier. Miss Seeton looked up. Now that was very interesting. Or, rather, it was interesting because it wasn't, so to speak. Though slightly unusual to meet an epicanthic fold to the eye in a rather longish head—a cephalic index of less than seventy-five, she should judge—when taken with the straight dark hair, the dark eyes, and the flattened cheekbones it became, though rather foreign, normal. Almost dull. Dull by comparison, that was. Quite different, naturally, to that other man—the head cashier who'd died—with his piercing light-blue eyes and fair wavy hair. But, of course, an identical formation. What a complete difference coloring could make. Without question a most interesting comparison. Unconsciously she reversed the filled-in slip and started making the comparison upon the back.

His business completed, the man at the front turned his head. Caught staring, Miss Seeton smiled uncertainly. The man's dark eyes narrowed; after a moment the lips below the thin black mustache stretched in answer and he came toward her.

"Miss Seeton, isn't it?" Surprised Miss Seeton nodded. "What luck," said the man. "I hope you won't think it rude, my speaking to you like this. You don't know me, but I've been awfully anxious to meet you."

Miss Seeton, who could think of no reply to this, said, "Oh?"

As the two people in front of her dispatched their business, the man stood to one side. Miss Seeton's turn came and she handed her slip and check to Mr. Jestin, who took them and said, "Thank you. Good morning, Miss Seeton. Warmer, isn't it?"

Miss Seeton countered this with "Good morning, Mr. Jestin, thank you. Yes, such a change." She turned.

"Allow me." The dark-eyed man picked up her shopping bag. Was she going to make a scene here in the bank or was she going to try being canny? She seemed to have a fancy for playing a lone hand—gave her more kudos, he supposed. He moved to the door. No question the old cow had rumbled him—her and her knowing smirk. His speaking first had thrown her. She hadn't expected that; could only look halfwitted and say, "Oh?" He held the door for her and waited. Probably meant to ask Jestin his name and address as soon as he was gone; but he wasn't going—not till she did. So she'd either have to come out into the open or start playing it his way. Miss Seeton passed him with a murmured "Thank you." He followed her out. If he could fool her into believing he hadn't twigged she was on to him she might play along—she seemed to think herself so clever—and he'd win out yet. She wanted his address. Well, give her a chance to find that out for a kickoff.

"So kind." Miss Seeton held her hand out for her shopping. He retained it.

"I wonder," he asked diffidently, "if you can spare the time, will you help me with a problem?"

"A problem?" Miss Seeton echoed in surprise.

Sarcasm, huh? Good. Going to play it solo, was she? Couldn't resist *Lone Woman Detective Captures Wanted Man*.

His mind, the cashier congratulated himself, was working brilliantly, meeting this emergency as it had met the previous one when Miss Seeton's presentation of her check had made him flee the bank and for a brief time had had him on the run. What the cashier did not realize was that his conscience had misinterpreted the evidence; had forced him to run when there was no immediate need to do so; had made him put his plan into operation while he was off balance; had been largely responsible for his committing two murders instead of the one for which he had allowed. Since his original plan had now been accomplished, his conscience appeared to feel itself quit of further obligation in the matter; or possibly in view of the result of its previous intervention it had quit while the going was good. Panic was now his only mentor. For a petty crook with a facile brain, an ill-founded conceit in his own acumen, and a serious lack of judgment when it came to long-term planning Panic is a dangerous companion. It can produce quick solutions to immediate crises, living from moment to moment without counting cost or consequence.

"I know it's cheek," he hurried on confidently, "but my car's here and I live fairly close, just on the outskirts of Brettenden up Les Marys' way. You see, it's not a matter I can talk about in the street or over coffee where people could listen. It's to do as you must've guessed with Superintendent Delphick. So if you would come back with me just for a short while I'd be awfully grateful. Of course, I'd drive you home."

"Well, really," said Miss Seeton, "I don't think I ..." He went to his car and opened the door. "Please, Miss Seeton. If it wasn't so important to me I wouldn't ask."

She hesitated. "Well ... I ..." What a strange man. One didn't, of course, like to appear rude. Or, again, unwilling to help. If, as he seemed to think, one could. Though in what way could one be of service to a complete stranger? On the other hand, they both used the same bank, which was, in a way, she supposed, an introduction. And then, again, Mr. Jestin had seemed to know him, so he must be all right. But one did wonder—although it was a little difficult to ask him since he'd said, perfectly understandably, that it was not a matter for discussion in public; which, of course, if it concerned Superintendent Delphick, one could see—quite how he thought one could help him. "Quite how," asked Miss Seeton, "do you think I can help you?"

Tongue like an adder. She could help him all right—by falling under the nearest bus, and well she knew it. Still holding the door invitingly he looked contrite: "I'm sorry, I know it's asking a lot of a stranger, but when you're in a state you lose the north a bit." This at least was true. The cashier had not only lost the north, but under Panic's guidance unwittingly had thrown away the compass. "Since you know the superintendent," he continued, "and with your knowledge of police work ..."

"My ...?" repeated Miss Seeton blankly. "I assure you I ..."

"Please," he interrupted. "I'd been thinking I ought to get on to Delphick about things—was actually going to ring up and make an appointment. Then meeting you at the bank seemed like the answer. You could tell me what I ought to do before I make more of an ass of myself than I have."

Somewhat to her surprise and without realizing quite how she came to be there, Miss Seeton found herself in the car and the door slammed, while this very insistent man ran round to jump into the driver's seat.

"Sir, sir ..."

The bank manager looked up. "It's usual to knock, Jestin, before bursting in."

"But, sir, we must get on to the police at once."

"The police?" The manager shuddered. "We've had quite enough of the police. Headquarters isn't pleased."

"But, sir," young Jestin practically danced in his excitement. His chance had come, as he had known it would. Placed by his father in the bank, a steady livelihood, secure and safe, the boy had eked out his romanticism in dreams. He worked conscientiously and well but, had this been the sum, frustration must have warped his nature. In compensation for a routine job young Jestin had aimed at self-education: he had read. He read all the books on which he could lay his hands to improve his knowledge of the banking world as he saw it and to prepare himself for those exigencies and demands that his role as cashier would one day make upon him. From his position behind the grill when he cashed a check—two pounds for Mrs. Furbelow—or corrected a paying-in slip—over three figures, Miss Enden who runs the Cosie Tea Rooms loses count—he knew full well the danger in which he stood. One day inevitably he would be held at gunpoint: all his reading told him so. In spite of top directives to hand over money and to take no risks, when that day came young Jestin was going to show them, show what and to whom was still uncertain, but show them he would. Convinced that his call to high endeavor must come, he continued with his studies and his readings: Crime, in hard covers from the lending library, in paperbacks from Smith & Son down the street. His time had now arrived. He knew the form, knew exactly what to do, and was exasperated that fuddyduddies like the manager, ill-read and worse-prepared, should be obstructing him.

"It's MissEss, sir," he explained, clinging to patience. "She tipped me the wink. It's him, she said so. Dead artful she was—he must've been holding a gun on her and I never saw. She never batted an eyelash, just said 'Such a change,' smooth as could be pretending she was talking of the weather, and handed me the drawing cool as you please on the back of her slip, knowing I'd cotton on. She's dead clever. And then went out with him just as they do on films and knowing he'll kill her and leaving it up to me." He swelled with pride. "She trusted me, you see. You must admit, sir, she's wonderful."—

The manager slapped his desk. "What, Jestin, are you talking about?"

"MissEss, sir—that is, Miss Seeton, sir. I told you." And he did: explained what had happened from his point of view; held out Miss Seeton's slip reverse side up. "There you are, sir, the spitting image. One with dark eyes, dark hair and a mustache—the other as he was. You can't mistake him. Can't think why I never saw it. But we must get the police, sir, or she's a goner. She left it up to me."

The manager frowned. Hysteria? And yet … Miss Seeton worked for Scotland Yard. Head office'd be furious. But if anything went wrong they'd take it out on him. Couldn't afford more trouble either way. He washed his hands. "If you choose to get in touch with the police about this scatter-brained idea of yours, you may. But it's on your own responsibility. If," he threatened, "you're stirring up a mare's nest with hornets in it, Jestin, I warn you I shall put in a report. You must do what you think best."

"Yes, sir." Jestin closed the door, raced to the telephone, and got through to the Brettenden police. "Police?" At least here he'd meet with quick response and understanding. "Code name, MissEss," he rapped out with professional enthusiasm.

"Your name?" inquired the phone. "And your address?"

"MissEss," repeated Jestin, "she's in trouble."

The phone was patient. "What name did you say, sir? And what's your address?"

"Miss Seeton," wailed Jestin, "her code's MissEss. She works for Scotland Yard. She got a message through to me. Her life's in danger."

"Miss Seeton, you say? With Scotland Yard? One moment, sir." The telephone and time stood still. A new voice on the line, calm, imperturbable. "Who's speaking, please?"

"It's Jestin from the bank—about MissEss."

"I understood you said Miss Seeton, sir."

"I did," cried Jestin. "Can't you understand, her life's in danger, there's no time to lose."

"Her life? In danger?" The telephone was surprised. "I see, sir. Quite. And from whom?"

"From our head cashier," yelled Jestin. "The one who's dead."

The telephone endured. "You say he's dead, sir?"

"Yes." Jestin almost screamed in his frustration. "He died the other day after killing all those children. He's back again and just gone off with her at gunpoint in a car."

"If you'd hold the line, sir," said the telephone. Another endless wait. The phone snapped back to life. "Ashford Police Headquarters. Chief Inspector Brinton speaking. Something about Miss Seeton, is it?"

Once more poor Jestin, disillusioned now and lost to hope, delivered his explanation: MissEss; the code; her drawings and her trust; how she was forced into a car at gunpoint; and, finally, under questioning, he actually divulged the name and address of his late colleague's new identity.

They drove up Virgin's Lane to Les Marys' in a silence which Miss Seeton sought to break. It was really very difficult to know quite what to say under the circumstances. He evidently didn't wish to discuss what troubled him until they reached their destination. On the other hand, to say nothing seemed a little rude. The weather—she looked out the window—was hardly an appropriate subject and—she looked at him—one mustn't, of course, be personal, but:

"You know," she observed, "the length of your head—the cephalic index of less than seventy-five, I mean—is interesting. In conjunction with the exterior epicanthic fold, that is. I can only remember seeing it once before. The cashier who used to be at the bank had it. Possibly you remember him?"

Possibly he did. Double-talking old witch. His voice was low and husky. "My brother," he said simply. Oh, how truly dreadful. So very tactless. She should have realized that there might be a connection. "That was the reason," he added brokenly, "I wanted your advice." Distressed, Miss Seeton said no more. They drove on, once again in silence.

On their arrival at the house he showed her the hall, the rooms on either side. Miss Seeton, who did not admire his taste, agreed that they were well appointed. The poor man seemed ill at ease and, considering the trouble his brother must have caused him, really one couldn't wonder.

How was he going to work this, now he'd got her here? She must have an accident; and she must have it pretty quick. But how? Panic reminded him the old cow painted didn't she? Of course. The cashier grasped the lifeline without thought. The roof: you could see for miles from there. She'd called to ask if she could study the view with the idea of painting it from there. He'd said he didn't mind; showed her the way up and left her to it. If she fell off it wasn't his lookout.

"To an artist like you," he suggested, "it's the view would be the thing. It's a bit of a way, but if you could manage to come up on to the roof I could show you." A good shove—and nobody could prove it wasn't an accident. "Also," he continued sadly, "it sounds a bit stupid, I suppose, but I'd find it easier to talk there in the open than here in the house." He stretched out a hand and gestured. "All this, you see, I'd meant to share with him."

Chastened, and determined not to make another gaffe, Miss Seeton followed him up the stairs. On the roof—flat, with a low parapet—Miss Seeton, rather out of breath, tried to admire the view and failed. In honesty she did her best.

"What a long way you can see," she said. Which was true, though the sight was dull. He led her to the parapet. She looked down. So very far. It made one giddy. Quickly she looked up again. He put his hand upon her shoulder. Really. A little familiar, thought Miss Seeton, though, of course, one must remember that the poor man was distressed.

A short burst upon a siren held them stationary, as a police car, blue light flashing, hurtled up the drive. Figures jumped out and ran toward the house, shouting and gesticulating. Practice improves. Miss Seeton undoubtedly was giving the patrol car practice and on this occasion they proved improvement, arriving before instead of after the event. More cars arriving; more men in uniform. Suddenly the grounds seemed full of the police. One aimed a loudspeaker at them and shouted through it with enthusiasm but without technique; the result was raucous, lively, unintelligible. Height and dizziness forgotten, Miss Seeton watched engrossed.

"Good gracious. There's Superintendent Delphick!" she exclaimed. "How very fortunate." She waved back in greeting to a waving hand below. "Such a very understanding man. So sympathetic. I'm sure that if you go down and talk to him you'll find that he'll do all he can to help. That is, I mean ..."

She stopped. This strange man wasn't listening. Just staring before him like someone in a trance.

He let go of her shoulder. Moved nearer to the parapet. Instinctively Miss Seeton put out her hand. So much too near the edge. So dangerous.

"You win," he muttered slowly. "All along the line. So this is the end. Of Maryse. Of everything. Of me."

"If you went down …?" Miss Seeton urged.

As in a dream he stepped upon the parapet, another step, a final, helpful nudge from Panic, and down indeed he went.

The fall deeply shocked the driver of the police car on which the body landed; it dented the car's roof and broke, among certain other things, the erstwhile cashier's neck.

Chapter 11

"All right, so she's ruined Saturday afternoon and my potatoes aren't in. If she must take over all our cases, decide we've got 'em wrong and it's up to her to put 'em right, why can't she do it hush-hush on the side? Just give me a jab in the ribs with her brolly and say, 'You've got it all cockeyed, chum.' No need to go skipping about the rooftops with a man we've buried, and then pushing him off and damaging a car." He caught Delphick's eye. "All right, so she didn't. Saw him walk off myself. But she might just as well've given him a shove." Chief Inspector Brinton unbuttoned his tunic and lay back in his chair. "I've done enough today for thirteen men. What with the coroner—very biting he was: most impressed that with all our modern scientific what-have-you we got the sexes right; but he's sick of issuing death certificates wrongly labeled. Wants to know who the charred stiff was. As if we knew—or ever will. Probably some tramp. We'll dig him up and put him on ice and do our best, but what can you expect? Can't issue a description of burned meat." He yawned and stretched. "Your Miss Seeton—can't you chain her up, Oracle; sit on her head, do anything, but for the love of Pete let's have the rest of the weekend off."

Delphick chuckled. "There's gratitude. She's tidied everything up for you, Chris, saved us a trial, and anyway you should be all right this evening—they've got a dance on in the village hall which will keep the locals occupied, and Miss Seeton's having dinner with the Colvedens: they thought it would help to take her mind off this morning's escapade. Incidentally, Sir George is offering young Hosigg the position of farm foreman under Nigel. Says he's a good type and reliable; sound mechanic. I hope the boy takes it, it strikes me as far better for him than the night lorry driving job."

"Good." Brinton sighed. "That leaves Plummergen all quiet and happy. Now—" He leaned forward and looked at the latest drawing lying on his desk. "You know, Oracle, with Miss Seeton's present output there's nothing between my office and the Tate. I could open it to the public and charge admission. But as to this," he flicked the sketch, "I can't agree with you. I know you explained it all to me in Greek, with para-this and psycho-that—we've got an inspector here who's just your glass of beer; natters about psycho stuff for hours, and all in the original Chinese—but me, I speak only two languages, English and basic. This picture says one thing to me: it says that one more stiff is coming up. I'm sending over our two pantywaists to keep an eye on the little perisher until we've nailed it down. And if they muck it like they did the Goffer kid, I'll fry 'em both for supper."

"Fair enough." Delphick stood. "That should cover things no matter which of us is right. You get your potatoes in tomorrow—and pray they don't get blight. And I'll get back to Plummergen and let's hope it all keeps fine. We'll sort things out on Monday."

The shed doors were open. Dick Quint was tinkering with his van. Doris had joined him: it seemed it wouldn't start; they both got in to try again. The engine caught. They shot through the gates, turned left toward the village, and were gone.

Bob fumed. They'd fooled him. Where were the men from Ashford who were supposed to be keeping watch? He used his walkie-talkie and reported the Quints' van was on the road, to be stopped on sight. Easing himself out from behind the bushes where he'd been lurking, he prepared to walk back to the George and Dragon. Quick footsteps behind him. Bob turned and shone his torch. A young man in a leather coat, a purple shirt, and a pink tie ran up to him; identified himself as D. C. Foxon, Ashford Division. Had the sergeant seen the Quints' kid brother? He'd been detailed to keep an eye on him but hadn't been able to raise him yet. Bob told him he didn't know; hadn't seen him; didn't think he was in the house, and was pretty sure he wasn't in the van.

"Then where'll I pick him up?" cried Foxon. "I got over here double quick but haven't set eyes on him. The chief'll have my hide if I slip up on this."

Bob suggested to ask Potter, the local constable. He might know. They left the common and walked down together.

Several cars and motorcycles lined the Street. Music was blaring from the village hall, set back on waste ground opposite the garage. A crowd of youths was milling round the entrance. Bob left his companion at the police station and continued on his way. Looked like Plummergen was going to make a night of it. At the George and Dragon, Delphick had just got in; Bob gave him his report. The superintendent went straight to the telephone, caught Brinton as he was leaving his office, and let him know the Quints were on the loose and patrol cars had been alerted. Also it seemed that the young brother had ducked from sight before one of the men detailed to watch him had arrived. Brinton blasphemed and said all right, so he'd stay on and wait developments; to keep him posted.

The vegetables were ready. Lady Colveden took a dish from the warming drawer. They could be dished up and left in there to keep warm. The chicken was almost done and with aluminum foil over it, that could wait. Miss Seeton was due any moment and they'd have time for a drink before dinner.

The kitchen door burst open and two masked black figures in cycling gear rushed in. Lady Colveden uttered a cry and dropped the dish.

"Enough from you." The taller of the figures put a pistol to her head.

"What's up, Meg? Did you …?" Sir George, in the doorway, stopped, stood rigid. Behind him Nigel gasped.

"One peep out of either of you and she gets it, see."

Pushing Lady Colveden in front of him, the man with the pistol forced them out of the kitchen into the hall. The second black figure followed, tried two doors, left the second open, took the key from the lock and gestured. The Colvedens were crowded in; the door was slammed and locked.

It was very kind of Sir George and Lady Colveden to invite her to dinner; the kinder in that one suspected that Lady Colveden feared one might be brooding. Which, of course, was ridiculous. This morning's affair had been all very distressing, naturally. But it was not, after all, as if one had known the man; nor, from the little one had seen of him, would one have wished to. That length of head—in conjunction, of course, with the eyefold—did not, in her experience, she was afraid, denote the best of characters. The police had taken it for granted that he was the bank cashier which, she supposed, might well be true. In fact they had proved it to their satisfaction by taking his fingerprints and removing his contact lenses. Such a clever invention—from Germany, she understood; though they had them in England too. And his mustache, a false one, had come off, they said, which proved their point. They—the police, that was—had also taken it for granted that she knew too; and had known all along. Which seemed a little strange. How should she have? Indeed how could she have? But, in view of their conviction and the fact that they were very busy at the time and had appeared to be so worried about one's being on the roof, one hadn't liked to insist upon it, but actually, of course, the man had said he was the other's brother. It was all very complicated and frankly not a thing to dwell on. The Colveden family were always so very thoughtful, so kind and generous, that one would like to feel that there was something one could do in return. Though really, when one considered, it was a little difficult to imagine what. Filled with kind thoughts and good intentions Miss Seeton set out.

How odd. The porch light wasn't on. At Rytham Hall the porch light was always on, she understood, until they went to bed. But tonight it wasn't. In fact there were no lights showing anywhere. Miss Seeton groped her way forward. So very careless to have forgotten to remember to put a new flashlight battery on one's shopping list this morning.

Perhaps they were out; though it seemed unlike them and a little strange. At all events perhaps one had better ring the bell. It was one of those handle things, she recollected, that pulled. Somewhere on the right, wasn't it? Or was it on the left? Miss Seeton felt about and failed to find it. She did, however, find the door open. The front door open? On a cold night like this? Now surely that was wrong. One didn't like to intrude in people's houses. But, on the other hand … Perhaps if one just switched on a light to make sure that all was well. She stroked the wall. No light switch came to hand. Miss Seeton smelled the dinner cooking. This reassured her. Perhaps if one found one's way to the kitchen? Now that, she recalled, was down the passage, on the right, just past the stairs. Pointing her umbrella before her as a feeler, she tiptoed forward. A moment later the umbrella point sank into something soft which gasped.

"Oh," said Miss Seeton, "I do beg your pardon."

There was a banshee wail of terror, a swirl of movement, and someone shot past her and through the open doorway; there was the sound of running footsteps on the drive. Above her, a clatter as something fell and junkled down the stairs. Feet pounded down in hot pursuit, went thudding past her in the darkness, receding as they followed their companion. The noise of two engines starting up; they roared; then dwindled in the distance.

Somewhere there was banging; there were cries. Really, thought Miss Seeton, so like the post office. There must, she was certain now, be something very wrong. If only she could see. Her umbrella touched a table. She put out her hand to pat the surface. She patted several objects. There might be … there was—a table lamp. She switched it on. The banging,

Miss Seeton located, came from behind a door on her right, just near the kitchen. She tried the handle. It was locked. She turned the key. Out surged Sir George and Nigel followed by Lady Colveden.

"I'm so sorry," apologized Miss Seeton, "if I've been a little long. I couldn't find a light."

"I've always said," said Lady Colveden, "that keys are old-fashioned. It should have a bolt—on the inside. Safer and more practical." She put the key back into place and closed the door.

"More to the point," observed her son, "to call the plumber in and make it a three-seater."

They dispensed with the formalities and had their dinner by the drawing-room fire on trays. Sir George rang the police to let them know of the attempted burglary. No, nothing taken. Miss Seeton had had the whole affair in hand, sorted the thieves out, and sent 'em packing. The silver and stuff was in a sack at the bottom of the stairs. Only damage he could see was one dish: vegetable—smashed; and one mirror: hand, in silver—cracked. Should bring bad luck to whoever'd tried it on.

It had. The Quints had been caught, he was informed. A farmer who was helping to deliver a sick cow in calf had noticed a strange van parked behind some outbuildings and reported it. The police had identified it as Quint's, found tire marks and oil drips on the floor and two spare pairs of black overalls hanging on some pegs. They had laid an ambush and when the Quints had returned on motorcycles, they'd been arrested. Their alibi for the P.O. job was bust. The Quint woman seemed in a bad way; babbling about hoodoo or voodoo or some such; but the cow and calf were doing well. The deaf-and-dumb brother was missing; they were looking for him.

A telephone call from Miss Treeves, to say that a lot of boys from Ashford had come over and started a disturbance at the dance. They were fighting in the Street. Arthur was out; she was a little worried. Nigel set off at once to see what he could do. Sir George told her that as a local justice he wouldn't like to interfere unless they asked him, in case the village might resent it; but if things started to look serious … Would she keep in touch? She would. Miss Treeves rang off, relieved.

Miss Seeton rose to leave. She and her hosts parted with mutual expressions of gratitude and good will. Lady Colveden lent her a flashlight and persuaded her to take the footpath opposite, which led down to the towpath alongside the canal. That would bring her home the back way through her garden. Although there was nothing to worry about now that the burglars had been caught, if there was trouble in the Street it might be wiser, she explained.

The trouble in the Street was rampant. The Ashford Choppers, true to their arrangement with Dick Quint, had arrived in joyous form and fettle. They had spent a few minutes dancing in the village hall to show their peaceable intent; but this unnatural behavior had lasted only so long as it took to pick a local girl, barge into her roughly, quite by accident and, when her swain protested, to stamp upon his feet. The ensuing fight developed quickly into a free-for-all, surged from the hall onto the Street, which was the Choppers' element, and now fists were thudding, staves were thwacking, stones were flying, there was the glint of knives.

The vicar stopped on his way home to watch the foray with indulgence. Youth was the time for spirits. He remembered how, as a young divine, he'd dropped an earwig down a lady's neck at a church outing; so boisterous he had been. He viewed the battlefield again; Saturday night, and youth was at the helm; no harm, of course; just braggadocio, providing they did not keep it up too late disturbing people's sleep. With a tolerant smile he turned to go. Near him Stan Bloomer was brought to knee, blood running from his cheek.

"Stan," cried the vicar, "what are you doing here? You're too old for this."

"Them Ashford lot," gasped Stan, " 'm's breaking up t'village."

The vicar looked again. True. Strangers. Benevolence faded from his face as anger rose. Stan was right; this was no horseplay, this was serious. This was veritable war. All his vexation against the recent happenings boiled up, boiled over. This he'd stop; he'd stop it personally. He strode into their midst.

"Stop this," he thundered. No one heard. "All of you, stop this at once, I say." No one took heed. A stave cracked on his ankle, a stone removed his hat. Armed warfare. They were armed. Then so would he be. He trotted to the vicarage, entered his armory, and reviewed his weapons. A scythe? A billhook? No, too dangerous. A hoe? He grasped its handle, felt the sharpened end. It might cause damage. Ah, this—the perfect antidote. He seized his new yard broom, red plastic bristles in spiked array. He'd lost his hat. Upon a beam hung by its chinstrap, mushroom shaped, his wartime warden's helmet, crown drilled for drainage. It held geranium plants. He tipped them out and clamped it on his head. His face earthstreaked and cobwebby he left the potting shed. Stones. They were throwing stones. He'd need a shield. He snatched the dustbin lid as he went by. Returning to the Street thus awesomely caparisoned he galloped to the fray.

Brinton had kept Delphick posted and had advised him of the Quints' arrest. Seeing the commotion brewing on the Street, with the village forces hopelessly outnumbered, Delphick had called for reinforcements. Meanwhile he had gone with Bob to lend his authority in quelling the disturbance. In such a melee, where the invaders had uprooted staves from the fence around the village hall to use for distance work, keeping their own armory of wrenches, chains, and knives for infighting, authority was at a discount and Delphick found himself reduced in rank to soldier of the line.

Mel watching from her bedroom window at the inn sized up the situation. Wow—so this was country life. She put on low-heeled shoes, grabbed a long-strapped totebag and ran downstairs. In the hall a brass doorstop attracted her. The ideal thing. She dropped it in the handbag and swung it experimentally. That should do. Well slung, that should settle somebody. She joined the combatants.

A tin helmet bobbed amidst the tumult. It vanished. The vicar was down. Was up again, his shield held high. He waved his broom in triumph; another Ashford rough had bitten bristle. Beside him Len Hosigg with a captured stave belabored bravely.

Delphick was down: towering, Bob straddled him. Three Choppers, hung round the broad back and shoulders, were bringing him slowly to his knees. Detective Foxon leaping to his assistance accounted for one of them. Bob gripped another by the leg and with a heave flung him to P. C. Potter who received him, twisted him round and handcuffed him. The third assailant Bob hauled off his shoulder, threw him on the ground and stood on him. As Delphick got to his feet

Bob turned to thank his helper but the leather coat, slashed open down the back, the pink tie awry, was threshing its way toward the vicar, intent on rescue work.

"All right, sir?"

"Yes," said Delphick. An ugly bruise was swelling round the ragged gash on his temple from a piece of wrench work. "Try and form up in line with Potter. See if we can sweep 'em back."

The noise had brought Miss Wicks out to her garden. Strangers? Scrapping? Scandalous. She'd sort them, she decided. She titupped to her toolshed and came back trailing coils of hose, connected one end to the outside tap and, with the nozzle pointed like a gun, advanced to her front gate. Mel was worming her way to where Nigel, losing ground, was engaged with a lout wearing a bicycle chain round his fist as knuckleduster. The lout braced for a well-placed kick and was joined by an ally brandishing a knife. Carefully Miss Wicks took aim; she turned the nozzle tap. Nigel received the impact in his ear. Tst, tst—she'd not allowed for wind. While Nigel was bemused, knife raised, his opponent whooped and jumped. Miss Wicks resighted, raised the nozzle, and got him in full whoop and open-mouthed. He choked, erupted water like a whale, and Nigel floored him; bent to retrieve the knife. Meanwhile his friend, recovered from the kick, brought his mailed fist down for a rabbit punch on Nigel's exposed neck. Mel reached them, swung her weighted bag, and landed it full in the lout's face. That was the end of him.

Miss Treeves's second telephone call to Rytham Hall was in the nature of a trumpet call, an urgent call to arms. Sir George hurried down the passage to the gun room, picked his weapon, and collected ammunition. He drove the big station wagon from the garage, then stopped it in the drive as Lady Colveden ran up to him.

He shook his head. "No, Meg. Not a show for women."

"Don't be silly, George." She climbed in and slammed the door. "If you think I'm going to stay here on my own to be locked up in the lavatory again … Besides, Nigel says I rattle—so I will. You know when you used to go to football matches. I thought—it's sure to be in the attic, and it was." She settled back in triumph as Sir George engaged the gear.

* * *

Miss Seeton locked the door in the wall behind her. So good of Lady Colveden to lend the flashlight. Although one knew exactly where the bushes were and, naturally, the beds, somehow in the dark they shifted round a bit and took one by surprise. She crossed the lawn toward the kitchen door. Behind her something moved. She turned quickly and the beam showed a boyish face, a guileless smile, a small slight figure. The light glinted on wire which dangled in his hand: he swung it slowly to and fro. Miss Seeton stepped back; he forward. It would be silly to pretend one wasn't frightened because, of course, one was. Very. It would be no good speaking, trying to reason with him. And, in any case, he couldn't hear. She moved again: so did he; savoring. Her heel hit something, stopping her. There shouldn't be … Oh, yes. The garden roller. She took a step sideways to avoid it. He sidestepped, keeping her in line … She staggered and nearly fell, with her umbrella's ferrule wedged behind the chock. The chock shifted, then flipped free. She stumbled clear.

Released from its impediment the roller inclined its handle gracefully. It crunched the gravel as it trundled forward, lumbered majestically across the path to reach the lawn and, handle waving, gathered speed. Miss Seeton watched aghast. Oh dear, there'd be an accident. The youth, his attention only fixed on her, crouched and sprang. She hooked her umbrella in the roller's frame and pulled. The roller took no notice: took the umbrella which, flung sideways as it slipped from her grasp, caught the youth's legs as he jumped for her and brought him down. Seeing his danger, trying to save him, Miss Seeton dropped the flashlight and grabbed the flailing handle, pulled with all her strength. The roller swerved: there was a noise like a branch snapping, a babbling, an obstructed scream. Then all was quiet as, mission accomplished, the roller came to rest upon its victim. Miss Seeton rescued the flashlight and looked at the small, unconscious form—one leg distorted, trapped beneath the weight. She looked at the roller, tugged. She couldn't shift it.

"Don't move," she said. "Stay here and keep quite still. I'll go for help." She picked up her umbrella, turned and ran.

* * *

Training and organization told. The police line was making headway. Foxon had joined them; Stan Bloomer, seeing their intent, had rounded up some other men to help extend the line which had formed at the end of the Street before Miss Seeton's cottage. Delphick and Foxon had taken the center, supported by the locals; Potter and Sergeant Ranger held the flanks. Step by step the line was making progress; slowly the few were pushing back the many.

Heedless of what was going on about her, intent upon her mission, Miss Seeton ran into the Street. The first man she saw was P.C. Potter.

"Oh, Mr. Potter," she exclaimed, "please come at once. There's been an accident."

Potter turned his head; a stone hit it and he subsided at her feet. Shorn of one wing support the locals wavered, the police line broke. Miss Seeton stared about her in dismay. The lights from the houses showed little from a distance but a jostling, cursing throng. But Mr. Potter ... He might be trodded on. She knelt, took Potter's head upon her lap. More stones came winging. This was outrageous. Didn't they realize someone might get hurt? She put up her umbrella.

A switch was pressed: twin searchlights flared suddenly from behind the villagers, cutting a swath through the maelstrom, dazzling the attackers. A pistol shot. Another. And again. The chatter of machine-gun fire. The home team parted ranks to allow passage for their commander in chief and the huge car roared forward in low gear with Sir George, his left hand on the wheel, his right protruding from the driver's window, firing blanks from his starter's pistol, Lady Colveden at his side producing short bursts on a wooden rattle.

The Ashford Chopper gang was disconcerted. It is enjoyable to fight anonymously in the dark with weapons and with numbers on your side. It is not enjoyable, nor is it fair, to fight when bathed in light nor to find that your opponent has called on unknown reinforcements equipped with better weapons than your own. Knives, knuckledusters, blackjacks, and any honored form of thuggery is permissible. Armed retaliation, by the other side, is out of bounds.

Some hesitated, at a loss; gave ground. Some went for their bikes. The flight became a rout, then consternation, when they found they could not flee. Down the Street in orderly array, one leading, the others two abreast, came five police cars. Men spilled out of them to man the sidewalks and to block escape. The attitude of the invaders changed. They stood morose and silent, waiting. They'd leave it, as they always did, for counsel to explain in court: how they were misunderstood and put upon and never did a thing except to defend themselves and try to stop the fight when others went for them and for no sort of reason they could see.

Only one incident marred the Law's arrival. Miss Wicks, marking more cars coming from the Ashford Road and not noticing the blue lamps flashing till too late, fired with enthusiasm. Blinded by hose spray on his windshield, the driver of the leading car collided with Sir George's. Brinton got out enraged.

He and Delphick organized the mopping up: an ambulance was coming and a van to collect the "bag." The local casualties were to be sent to Knight's nursing home for treatment: with Sir George—three generals at the end of a campaign—they paced the battlefield, assessing damage.

A light rain was falling. Lady Colveden glanced up; she frowned and looked around, then left the car and crossed the Street. She took the hose from Miss Wicks's unresisting hand, turned off the nozzle tap and gave it back. The light rain stopped.

Foxon came to Brinton and reported.

"I've located the Quints' kid brother, sir. He's in Miss Seeton's garden at the back. She's dropped her garden roller on him to hold him there. Looks in a bad way. I think his leg's a goner."

"Right, then we'll pick him up." Brinton scanned his subordinate: the half of one trouser leg was gone, the other torn; his bare torso was decorated with a necklace of tattered strips of leather, purple silk and pink. "Who told you you could come here and dance starkers in the Street?" he growled. Foxon's lips parted, a tooth was missing. "So all right." Brinton called a police driver. He pointed to Foxon. "Take these bits and pieces to the hospital and see if they can mend 'em. And all right," he called after him, "so you'll need new clothes. If you must have 'em fancy, have 'em fancy, just don't let me see 'em, and I'll sign the chit." Gap-toothed and grinning Foxon was led away. Brinton felt vindicated. So he'd been wrong about the Choppers, but still, all right, they'd turned up in the end. And this little excursion coming pat with the Quints' last throw at burglary was too much to swallow as coincidence. Swallow? He wouldn't try. He'd have a go at them and at the Quints until he'd proved connection, and then for once the Choppers'd be up on a charge they couldn't wriggle out of. Mouthpiece or no mouthpiece the magistrate would have to take some notice, get 'em sent to Assize, and the Force could look forward to a few months' rest from 'em. Brinton turned to Delphick; noted the bleeding gash. "You look like you could do with sewing up."

Delphick laughed. "I'll get myself stitched at Dr. Knight's. At least, Chris, all the rest's sewn up. We've got the killer, got the raiders, and you've got your cashier. One way and another our Miss Seeton's bagged the lot for us."

Brinton snuffed. "Chummies are chummies the world over—they never learn. Four things in life you shouldn't try to buck. All right, fate's one of 'em. She's the other three."

* * *

From the *Daily Negative*—April 1

THE PEACE OF THE ENGLISH COUNTRYSIDE
by our correspondent from the front

*

Piece 4. *The Battle of Plummergen*

In the placid, peaceful depths of this tranquil corner of Old England the slumberous monotony of our rustic existence flows on at reckless pace …

… that it was a station wagon, but I was there and can only describe it as it seemed to me at the time: a monster tank, a dreadnought, a very battleship on wheels, guns blazing from every port. Sir George Colveden was at the helm, his gallant wife standing to her guns, as they came to the relief of the beleaguered inhabitants.

But bravely as we fought in the Battle of Plummergen, though many of us fell, fell over, some wounded; though the enemy was routed, to be rounded up and removed by the police, the main issue of all that we fought for was decided in a quiet garden behind an Old World cottage. There, in the darkness of the lawn, the only illumination the gleam of a flashlight, a small elderly lady came face to face with the seventeen-year-old youth who is alleged to have terrorized the whole country; the youth now in the hands of the police under arrest on a charge of murdering six children. Bravely she faced him undaunted, but not alone. As he leaped to the attack, her intrepid Brolly, working spoke-in-wheel with her garden roller, moved to her defense. With a lightning stroke the Brolly tripped him and brought him low and her guardian roller, with perfect timing, executed the *coup de grâce* and pinned him to the ground.

This tiny village gives the lead to the whole nation. For who shall say this country now is finished, this island of ours, this England, where such spirit still prevails, where garden rollers still stand sentinel, umbrellas still abound?

Amelita Forby
Knight's Nursing Home, Brettenden Road
Plummergen, Kent

(No flowers by request. We're a little overcrowded here at the moment.)

Preview

It's practically a Royal Marriage! The highly eligible son of Miss Seeton's old friends Sir George and Lady Colveden has wed the daughter of a French count.

Miss Seeton lends her talents to the village scheme to create a quilted 'Bayeux Tapestry' for Nigel and his bride. But her intuitive sketches reveal a startlingly different perspective—involving buried Nazi secrets, and links to a murdered diplomat and a South American dictator …

Serene amidst every kind of skulduggery, this eccentric English spinster steps in where Scotland Yard stumbles, armed with nothing more than her sketchpad and umbrella!

The new Miss Seeton mystery

COMING SOON!

About the Miss Seeton series

Retired art teacher Miss Seeton steps in where Scotland Yard stumbles. Armed with only her sketch pad and umbrella, she is every inch an eccentric English spinster and at every turn the most lovable and unlikely master of detection.

Further titles in the series—

Picture Miss Seeton
A night at the opera strikes a chord of danger when Miss Seeton witnesses a murder … and paints a portrait of the killer.

Miss Seeton Draws the Line
Miss Seeton is enlisted by Scotland Yard when her paintings of a little girl turn the young subject into a model for murder.

Witch Miss Seeton
Double, double, toil and trouble sweep through the village when Miss Seeton goes undercover … to investigate a local witches' coven!

Miss Seeton Sings
Miss Seeton boards the wrong plane and lands amidst a gang of European counterfeiters. One false note, and her new destination is deadly indeed.

Odds on Miss Seeton
Miss Seeton in diamonds and furs at the roulette table? It's all a clever disguise for the high-rolling spinster … but the game of money and murder is all too real.

Miss Seeton, By Appointment
Miss Seeton is off to Buckingham Palace on a secret mission—but to foil a jewel heist, she must risk losing the Queen's head … and her own neck!

Advantage, Miss Seeton

Miss Seeton's summer outing to a tennis match serves up more than expected when Britain's up-and-coming female tennis star is hounded by mysterious death threats.

Miss Seeton at the Helm

Miss Seeton takes a whirlwind cruise to the Mediterranean—bound for disaster. A murder on board leads the seafaring sleuth into some very stormy waters.

Miss Seeton Cracks the Case

It's highway robbery for the innocent passengers of a motor coach tour. When Miss Seeton sketches the roadside bandits, she becomes a moving target herself.

Miss Seeton Paints the Town

The Best Kept Village Competition inspires Miss Seeton's most unusual artwork—a burning cottage—and clears the smoke of suspicion in a series of local fires.

Hands Up, Miss Seeton

The gentle Miss Seeton? A thief? A preposterous notion—until she's accused of helping a pickpocket ... and stumbles into a nest of crime.

Miss Seeton by Moonlight

Scotland Yard borrows one of Miss Seeton's paintings to bait an art thief ... when suddenly a *second* thief strikes.

Miss Seeton Rocks the Cradle

It takes all of Miss Seeton's best instincts—maternal and otherwise—to solve a crime that's hardly child's play.

Miss Seeton Goes to Bat

Miss Seeton's in on the action when a cricket game leads to mayhem in the village of Plummergen ... and gives her a shot at smashing Britain's most baffling burglary ring.

Miss Seeton Plants Suspicion

Miss Seeton was tending her garden when a local youth was arrested for murder. Now she has to find out who's really at the root of the crime.

Starring Miss Seeton

Miss Seeton's playing a backstage role in the village's annual Christmas pageant. But the real drama is behind the scenes ... when the next act turns out to be murder!

Miss Seeton Undercover

The village is abuzz, as a TV crew searches for a rare apple, the Plummergen Peculier—while police hunt a murderous thief ... and with Miss Seeton at the centre of it all.

Miss Seeton Rules

Royalty comes to Plummergen, and the villagers are plotting a grand impression. But when Princess Georgina goes missing, Miss Seeton herself has questions to answer.

Sold to Miss Seeton

Miss Seeton accidentally buys a mysterious antique box at auction ... and finds herself crossing paths with some very dangerous characters!

Sweet Miss Seeton

Miss Seeton is stalked by a confectionary sculptor, just as a spate of suspicious deaths among the village's elderly residents calls for her attention.

Bonjour, Miss Seeton

After a trip to explore the French countryside, a case of murder awaits Miss Seeton back in the village ... and a shocking revelation.

Miss Seeton's Finest Hour

War-time England, and a young Miss Emily Seeton's suspicious sketches call her loyalty into question—until she is recruited to uncover a case of sabotage.

About the author

Heron Carvic was an actor and writer, most recognisable today for his voice portrayal of the character Gandalf in the first BBC Radio broadcast version of *The Hobbit*, and appearances in several television productions, including early series of *The Avengers* and *Dr Who*.

Born Geoffrey Richard William Harris in 1913, he held several early jobs including as an interior designer and florist, before developing a successful dramatic career and his public persona of Heron Carvic. He only started writing the Miss Seeton novels in the 1960s, after using her in a short story.

Heron Carvic died in a car accident in Kent in 1980.

Note from the Publisher

While he was alive, series creator Heron Carvic had tremendous fun imagining Emily Seeton and the supporting cast of characters.

In an enjoyable 1977 essay Carvic recalled how, after having first used her in three short stories, "Miss Seeton upped and demanded a book"—and that if "she wanted to satirize detective novels in general and elderly lady detectives in particular, he would let her have her head ..."

You can now **read one of those first Miss Seeton short stories and Heron Carvic's essay in full**, as well as receive updates on further releases in the series, by signing up at http://farragobooks.com/miss-seeton-signup